9 to 5

Falling for the boss...

They're working side by side, nine to five... But no matter how hard these couples try to keep their relationships strictly professional, romance is undeniably on the agenda!

But will a date in the office diary lead to an appointment at the altar?

Find out in this exciting miniseries!

The Tycoon's Reluctant Cinderella
by Therese Beharrie

Available now!

Dear Reader,

I've always sympathized with nonathletic people growing up in a family of active sporting enthusiasts. My heroine, Lauren Taylor, has no such prowess and enjoys reading and gentler activities like walking. As a teenager she rebelled against weekends spent attending her talented brother's games, and stayed home studying.

After gaining a master's degree in computing in Melbourne, she accepted a job in Sydney, defining herself as a computer problem investigator. Due to her high success rate she is personally requested by Matt Dalton in Adelaide. Her assignment is to find and fix the glitches affecting his father's failing company's system. One glance at their first meeting and she remembers a long-ago encounter related to a sporting event. She knows he's the type of man she avoids—privileged, self-assured and probably sport driven—yet can't deny his appeal.

Matt has deep-seated trust issues caused initially by knowledge of his father's infidelities. His experiences during his seven years in London enforced his belief that true love and happy-ever-afters were a myth, but he will admit to knowing a few couples who seem to be devoted to each other. He is convinced his instant attraction to Lauren and the niggle in his brain on occasions in her presence are due to his mental exhaustion. Pride in his family name and his father's worsening Alzheimer's make him determined to save the company from folding.

I loved taking Lauren and Matt on their sometimes bumpy journey leading to an emotional meeting when only heart-freeing confessions and honesty will bring them true happiness. I hope you enjoy reading their story.

Bella

A Bride for the Brooding Boss

Bella Bucannon

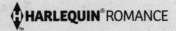

Recycling programs
for this product may
not exist in your area.

ISBN-13: 978-0-373-74427-5

A Bride for the Brooding Boss

First North American Publication 2017

Copyright © 2017 by Harriet Nichola Jarvis

Printed in U.S.A.

Bella Bucannon lives in a quiet northern suburb of Adelaide with her soul-mate husband, who loves and supports her in any endeavour. She enjoys walking, dining out and traveling. Bus tours or cruising with days at sea to relax, plot and write are top of her list. Apart from category romance, she also writes very short stories and poems for a local writing group. Bella believes joining RWA and SARA early in her writing journey was a major factor in her achievements.

Books by Bella Bucannon

Harlequin Romance

Bound by the Unborn Baby

Visit the Author Profile page
at Harlequin.com.

To my special husband, whose extra help enabled me to conquer the challenge of a deadline. To Brett for expert advice, once he and other friends had stopped laughing at the idea of technically inept Bella's heroine being a computer problem investigator. To the Paddocks Writing Group for support and encouragement, and to Flo for her advice and belief in me. My grateful thanks to you all.

CHAPTER ONE

LAUREN TAYLOR ALIGHTED from the taxi, smiling in surprise. A multi-storey glass and cement edifice had replaced the six-storey building with a bank at ground level she remembered from years ago.

Anticipation simmered through her veins. A rush job. Urgent—which usually meant challenging.

Her initial reaction to her employer's Monday morning call had been to refuse. She had managed to squeeze in a much-needed week off and had planned on some 'me' time—seeing movies, reading in the park, aimless walking… The promise of an additional week on completion of the assignment, plus a bonus, had won her over. A few days of Adelaide in March wouldn't be too hard to take.

The flight delay at Sydney airport the next afternoon meant it was three o'clock by the time she'd booked into her hotel and caught a taxi to the address. A quick phone call to a brusque Matthew Dalton raised some apprehension but he *was* the one with the critical dilemma.

Dalton Corporation's reception area on the eighteenth floor suited the building. A patterned, tiled floor drew the eyes to a curved redwood desk and up to the company name, elaborately carved in black on a gold background. Sadly the lack of human presence, along with the almost complete silence, detracted from the impact. The three doors in her sight were all shut.

Scrolling for the contact number she'd used earlier, she stopped at the sound of a crash from behind the second door along. Followed by a loud expletive in a woman's voice.

Lauren knocked and opened the door.

A blonde woman stood leaning across a desk, her hands shifting through a pile of papers, a harassed face turned towards Lauren. A document tray and its previous contents lay scattered on the floor.

'You want Mr Dalton.' Uttered as a hopeful statement. 'Sorry about this. I'm usually more organised. Last door on the left. Knock and wait. Good luck.'

Her words heightened Lauren's unease as she obeyed, instinctively smoothing down her hair before tapping on the door. The light flutter in her pulse at the raspy 'Come in' startled her. As did the unexpected allure in the deep guttural tone.

Without looking up, the man with a mobile held to his left ear gestured for her to enter and take the seat in front of his desk. Matthew Dalton was definitely under pressure. No jacket or tie, shirt unbuttoned at the top, and obviously raked through, thick chestnut-brown hair. He continued to write on a printed page in front of him, occasionally speaking in one-or two-word comments.

Lauren sat, frowning at the oblique angle of his huge desk to the wall-to-wall, floor-to-ceiling windows with an incredible view of the Adelaide Hills. Made of dark wood, it held only a desktop computer, keyboard, printer, land phone and stacked document trays. The only personal item was a plain blue coffee mug.

The man who'd requested her urgent presence swung to his right, flicking through pages spread on the desk extension. His easy fit in the high-back leather chair with wide arms suggested made to measure. And he needed a haircut.

She continued her scan, fascinated by the opulent differences from the usual offices where she was welcomed by lesser employees. From the soft leather lounge chairs by the windows to the built-in bar and extravagant coffee machine, this one had been designed to emphasise the power and success of the occupier.

The down light directly above his head picked up the red tints in his hair, and the embossed gold on his elegant black pen. She shrugged—exclusive taste didn't always equate with business acumen. If it did she might not be here.

Reception had been bare and unmanned, the blonde woman agitated. How bad *was* the company's situation?

Normally tuning out sounds was an ingrained

accomplishment. Today, nothing she tried quite prevented the gravelly timbre skittling across her skin, causing an unaccustomed warmth low in her abdomen. She steadied her breathing, mentally counting the seconds as they passed.

Then the man she believed to be a complete stranger flicked a glance her way. Instantly, with a chilling sensation gripping her heart, she was thrown back ten years to *that* night.

The dinner dance after a charity Australian Rules football game organised by interstate universities and held here in Adelaide. Limited professional players were allowed and her parents insisted the whole family come over in support when her elder brother agreed to represent Victoria.

The noisy function seemed full of dressed-to-kill young women draped over garrulous muscular males, many of whom twitched and pulled at the collars of their suits. Though only two or three years separated her from most of them, at sixteen it was a chasm of maturity and poise. Unfamiliar with the football scene and jargon, she blushed and stammered when any of them spoke to her.

Escaping from the hot, crowed room, she found a secluded spot outside, at the end of the long balcony. Hidden by tall potted plants, she gazed over the river wishing she were in her hotel room, or home in Melbourne. Or anywhere bar here.

'Hiding, huh? Don't like dancing?'

The owner of the throaty voice—too much en- thusiastic cheering?—was tall. Close. Much too close. The city lights behind him put his face in shadow.

She stepped back. The self-absorbed young men whose interests were limited to exercise, diet, sport, and the women these pursuits attracted held no appeal for her. Men like her brothers' friends who teasingly came on to her then laughed off her protests. Never serious or threatening, merely feeding their already inflated egos. Shy and un- comfortable in crowds, with a tendency to blush, she was fair game.

'I saw you slip out.' She detected a faint trace of beer on his breath as he spoke. When he took a step nearer, causing her to stiffen, a fresh ocean aroma overrode the alcohol. Not drunk, perhaps a little tipsy.

'We won, you should be celebrating. You do bar- rack for South Australia?' Doubt crept into the last few words, the resonance telling her he'd be more mature, maybe by two or three years, than she was. So why seek her out when there were so many girls his age inside?

'Y… Yes.' How could one word be so hard to say? How come her throat dried up, and her pulse raced? And why did she lie when she didn't care about the game at all?

He leant forward. 'I did kick two goals even if

I missed out on a medal. Surely I deserve a small prize.'

He *was* like all the others. Her disappointment sharpened her reply.

'I'm sure you won't be disappointed inside.'

'But an elusive prize is much more rewarding, don't you think?'

Before she could take in air to answer, he gently covered her lips with his.

And she hadn't been able to take that breath. Hadn't been able to move. Hadn't been able to think of anything except the smooth movement of his mouth on hers.

The urge to return the kiss—have *him* deepen the kiss—had shaken her. Terrified her. The quick kisses from the boys she knew were just being friendly had been gentle, nice. Never emotionally shattering.

Why did she sigh? Why were her lips complying, pressing against his, striving to be in sync? Until the tip of his tongue flicked out seeking entry and she panicked.

Frantically pulling away, she fled past him to the safety of the packed ballroom and a seat behind her parents and other adults in a remote corner. As she drank ice-cold water to wet her dry throat, she realised all she could recall was a glimpse of stunning midnight-blue eyes as his head had jerked back into the light.

* * *

The same midnight-blue eyes that had fleetingly met hers a moment ago.

Why was she so certain? She just knew.

Would he recognise *her*? He'd had a drink or two and it had been dark. She finally had a reason to be thankful for her mother's instructions to the hairdresser. Darker colouring with extensions woven into a fancy hairdo on top, plus salon make-up, had altered her appearance dramatically.

She'd been a naive teenager who'd panicked and run from an innocent kiss. He'd been an experienced young man who'd have known scores of willing women since.

Gratitude that she hadn't seen his face flowed through her veins as she studied the man to whom she'd attributed so many different features over the years in her daydreams. If, along with those memorable eyes, she'd imagined high cheekbones, a square firm jaw and full lips, she doubted she'd have slept at all. Even his lashes were thicker and darker than she'd pictured.

She dipped her head whenever he looked at her, wasn't ready for eye-to-eye contact. Forced steady breathing quelled her inner trembling.

Matt Dalton's mind ought to be totally focused on the information he was receiving. Instead his eyes kept straying to the brunette sitting rigid on her seat, politely ignoring him. The one who'd caused a tightening in his gut when he'd glanced up at her.

In an instant he'd noted the sweet curve of her cheek framed by shoulder-length light brown hair. If she hadn't dropped her gaze, he'd also know the colour of her eyes.

Shoot! He asked the caller to repeat the last two figures. Blocking her out, he carefully wrote them down. After ending the call, he clipped all the pages together, and dropped them into a tray.

He could now concentrate on this woman, and her technical rather than physical attributes. Her employer's high fees would be worth it if she found out what the heck had happened in the company's computer system.

'Ms Lauren Taylor?' He pulled a new document forward.

She turned, and guarded brown eyes met his.

He immediately wished they hadn't as a sharp pang of desire snapped through him and was instantly controlled. Women, regardless of shape, colouring or looks, were off his agenda for the foreseeable future. Probably longer. Betrayal made a man wary.

'Yes.' Hesitant with an undertone he didn't understand.

He'd requested her services on a recommendation, without any consideration of appearance or demeanour, which for him were unimportant. The female colleagues he'd associated with overseas were well groomed, very smart, and always willing to offer their opinions. His equal on every corporate level.

Lauren Taylor was neatly dressed in a crisp white blouse under a light grey trouser suit, and wore little make-up. With her reputation, she ought to project confidence, yet he sensed apprehension. Was it a natural consequence of her temporary assignments or the confidentiality clause creating a desire to keep a distance from company employees?

No, this ran deeper, was more personal. He cleared his thoughts, telling himself his sole interest was in her technical skills, conveniently discounting his two reactions towards her.

'I'm Matt Dalton. I contacted your employer because I'm told you're one of the best computer problem investigators. My friend's description. Was he exaggerating?'

A soft blush coloured her cheeks, and her eyes softened at the compliment. They were actually more hazel than brown with a hint of gold flecks, and framed by thick brown lashes. He growled internally at himself for again straying from his pressing predicament.

'I don't…I rarely fail.' She made a slight twitch of her shoulders as if fortifying her self-assurance.

He gave a short huff. 'Please don't let this be one of the times you do. How much information were you sent?'

'The email mentioned unexplained anomalies a regular audit failed to clarify.'

'Two, one internal, one external. The detectable errors were fixed but no one could explain the glitches or whatever they are, and I need answers fast.' Before his father's condition became public and the roof caved in.

'May I see the reports?' Again timidity, which didn't fit the profile he'd received, though to give her credit she didn't look away.

'In the top drawer of the desk you'll be using along with a summary of our expectations, file titles et cetera. I assume you can remember passwords.'

She frowned, making him realise how condescending he sounded. Was he coming over as too harsh, overbearing? Her impression of him wouldn't be good either.

'Staff turnover has been high in the last two years, sometimes sudden with no changeover training. Recently I found out passwords had been written down and kept in unlocked drawers.'

She waited, and he had the feeling he was being blamed for some personal misdemeanour. He decided he'd divulged as much as she needed to know to start. Anything else necessary, she'd learn as the assessment progressed.

'Most of the errors were from incorrectly entered data, exacerbated on occasion by amateur attempts to fix them. Apparently not too hard to find and correct if you know what you're doing.'

'But surely the accountant…?' Her hands fluttered then her fingers linked and fell back into her lap. 'Why weren't they picked up at the time?'

Damn, she was smart. And nervous.

'The long-term accountant left, and was replaced by a bookkeeper then another. Neither were very competent.'

Her eyes widened in surprise. For a second there was a faint elusive niggling deep in the recesses of his mind. As her lips parted he forestalled her words.

'I'd like you to analyse from July 2014 up to the present date. Everything your employer requested is in the adjacent office. How soon can you start?'

Too abrupt again but it was imperative he find out what had been going on. The sooner the better. Four weeks ago, at his original inspection of his father's company accounts, would have been best.

'If I can see the set-up now then I can begin early tomorrow morning. Being a short week because of Easter doesn't allow much time.

'Are two days enough?'

'Doubtful if I'm a last resort. I have a family commitment in Melbourne for the weekend then I'll come back.' She made it sound like an obligation rather than a pleasant reunion.

'That's acceptable.' He flicked his hands then put them on the edge of the desk to push to his feet.

'Human error and deliberate action are different. Is it the latter I'm searching for?'

He sank back into his chair. She was *too* smart.

Lauren had been in critical corporate situations before and recognised desperation, even when well hidden. This man was heading for breakdown. His taut muscles, firm set lips and weary dark eyes all pointed to extreme stress.

And her question had irritated him so he definitely suspected fraud, probably by someone he'd trusted. She certainly wasn't going to push it now. Not when she'd behaved like the skittish child she'd thought she'd conquered years ago.

'I won't make guarantees I might not be able to keep. I can only promise to do my best. Having the straightforward errors already adjusted helps.'

He relaxed a little, and his lips curved at the corners, almost but not quite forming a smile.

'Thank you.'

He rose to an impressive height, letting his chair roll away, indicating a door to her left.

'Through here.'

Lauren picked up her shoulder bag and followed, wishing she were one of those women who were comfortable in killer heels all day. And an inch or two taller. Having to tilt her head gave him the advantage. When he suddenly stopped and turned, her throat tightened at the vague familiarity of his cologne. Not the same one, surely? Yet she recognised it, had never forgotten it. And this close, the lines around his mouth and eyes were much more discernible.

'I apologise. I should have offered you a coffee. Do you—?'

'No. No, thank you.' The sooner she was out of his presence, the better. Then she could breathe and regroup. 'You're obviously busy.'

His relief at such a minor point enforced her opinion of the strain he was under.

'Like you wouldn't believe. Any answers you find will be extremely welcome.'

He opened the door and ushered her in, the light touch of his fingers on her back shooting tingles up and down her spine, spreading heat as they went. Unwarranted yet strangely exciting.

The décor in the much smaller room matched his office, and included two identical armchairs by the window. But the position of the desk was wrong, standing out from the wall facing the door they'd entered. She walked round to check the two desktops and a keyboard, all wired up ready to go. He followed, stopping within touching distance.

'Your employer asked for the duplication. Easier for comparisons, huh?'

'Much. What's the password?'

He told her. While she activated the computer, he removed a blue folder from the drawer, and placed it on the desk.

'Anything else you require?'

'I'll need a copy of the report for highlighting and a writing pad for notes.'

'Help yourself to anything in the cupboard. The copier is in Joanne's office off reception.'

'The blonde lady?'

'Yes, currently we don't have a receptionist. If you have any questions regarding your task ask me. If it's office related Joanne or any one of the other five employees can help.'

He walked out, not giving her a chance to say thank you, leaving his heady sea-spray aroma behind. Did he treat everyone in the same offhand manner?

Lauren felt like pounding the desk. She'd handled ruder employers who'd been under less pressure with poise and conviction. I'm-the-boss males with autocratic, archaic, even on occasion sexist, views were certainly not an endangered species. It didn't wash with her. They were in a predicament and she was the solution so she made it clear: no respect and she walked.

The personal aspect here had shaken her composure, giving the impression she doubted her abilities. She'd show him. Tomorrow she'd be the perfect detached computer specialist.

She selected stationery from the cupboard, skim-read the printed files, then spent ten minutes perusing the computer data prior to closing down. The few pertinent notes she'd written would save time in the morning.

Carrying the audit reports, she tried the door leading to the corridor. Finding it locked, she went into Matt Dalton's office. He was standing, sorting papers on his desk. His gaze was less than friendly to someone he'd hired to solve his problems.

'I'll copy these then I'll be leaving. What time is the office open in the morning?' Polite and stilted, following his lead. The fizz in her stomach could and *would* be controlled.

'I'm here from seven. Do you need transport?'

'I'll sort that out.'

'Good.' He returned to his papers.

She swung away, heat flooding her from head to feet at his dismissive action. All her fantasies came crashing down. Spoilt, rich, I-can-take-what-I-want teenager had become arrogant, treat-hired-staff-with-disdain boss. Was that why people had left without notice? She'd never wished bad karma on anyone, but she was coming close today!

Long deep breaths as she went out helped to settle her stomach and stop the trembling of her hands.

Before re-entering Mr Dalton's office, printouts in hand, she reinforced her prime rule of contract work. Never, never, ever get involved. Someone always ended up heartbroken.

Swearing the oath was easy. Sticking to it when confronted with those hypnotic blue eyes that invited her to confess her innermost secrets was tougher than she'd expected. Especially when his lips curled into a half-smile as he said goodbye.

She stabbed at the ground-floor button, angry that she'd smiled back, dismayed that even his small polite gesture had weakened her resolve. The thrill of the chase ought to be in his computer files, not in dreaming of— She wouldn't dream of anything. Especially not midnight-blue eyes, firm jaws or light touches that sent emotions into a frenzy.

CHAPTER TWO

MATT STARED AT the open doorway, perplexed by his reactions to a woman so unlike the outgoing, assured females he usually favoured. He raked his fingers through his hair. They were strangers, so why the censure in her alluring eyes when they'd met? It irked. It shouldn't have affected his attitude but he knew he'd been less than welcoming.

His finding her delicate perfume enchanting was also disconcerting. And she'd stiffened when he'd touched her. Had she felt the zing too? Please not. He had enough complications to deal with already.

Would it make her job easier if she knew the whole story? Loath to reveal family secrets to outsiders, he'd tell her only if it became relevant to her succeeding. Despite his friend's glowing report, he'd been less than impressed.

Dalton Corporation was in trouble. His only choice was to trust her on the corporate level. He had little reason to trust her, or any other woman, personally. Especially as her manner said she'd judged him for some transgression made by someone else.

Had she suffered the same indignity as he had? The soul-crushing realisation that you'd been used and played for a fool. The embarrassment of how

close you'd come to committing to someone un-
worthy, incapable of fidelity or honesty.

The dark-haired image that flared took him by
surprise. Any affection he'd felt for Christine had
died when she'd proved faithless. He hadn't seen
her since he'd walked out of her apartment for the
last time after telling her the relationship was over,
and why. He'd rarely thought of her either.

They'd both spent nights in each other's homes
but he'd held back from inviting her to live with
him. Looking back that should have been a red
flag that he had misgivings. Thankfully he'd told
no one of his plans to propose to her.

Admitting he'd been stupid for assuming mutual
friends and lifestyle expectations would be a good
basis for a modern marriage hadn't been easy. He
wasn't sure he'd ever consider that life-changing
step again.

God, he hated being here handling this mess.
He'd hated even more being in London where people gave him sympathetic looks and wondered
what had happened.

Letting out a heartfelt oath, he banished both
women from his mind. There were emails to read
and respond to, and he'd promised his mother he'd
be there for dinner. He grabbed his coffee mug, feeling the urgent necessity for another caffeine boost.

Nearly two hours later he pulled into the kerb outside his parents' house, switching off the engine to

give himself time to prepare for the evening ahead. He regretted the loss of unwavering respect for his parents, wished he'd never found out his father had been having affairs. He'd lost a small part of himself when he'd come home that evening nine years ago, and had never been able to obliterate what he overheard from his mind.

'I suppose this one's as gullible as the rest and believes she has a future with you. How many more, Marcus?'

'Man wasn't meant to be monogamous. If you want a divorce, be prepared to lower your standard of living.'

'Why should I suffer for your indiscretions? I'm giving up nothing.'

Somehow his mother's acceptance of his father's infidelities made her complicit. In disbelief he'd fled to his room, changed into a tracksuit and taken off, pounding the footpath trying to drive what he'd heard from his mind. His hero had fallen. He'd returned to a silent, dark house where, for him, nothing would ever be the same.

He scowled, thumping the wheel with an open hand. He'd always been confident, sure of himself and his judgement of cheating and affairs. Now he felt remorse as his father had turned into a stranger who'd made drastic mistakes in the last eighteen months, sending Dalton Corporation on a downhill path.

Pride dictated he fix those glitches and return the company to profit status, along with preserving its good name. Only then could he consider his own future, and for that he'd need a clear head. The only people he'd give consideration to would be family and his partners in London.

He started the engine, and drove through the elaborate gates, grimacing as he entered the luxurious house. This was his father's dream, a symbol of wealth and prestige, bought during Matt's absence abroad. He hadn't told his mother their financial status was in jeopardy. If Lauren Taylor was as good as her reputation, and he'd inherited any of his father's entrepreneurial skills, he might never have to.

Adelaide had a different vibe from the city Lauren remembered. Not that she'd seen much of the metropolitan area when she'd lived here, or much of anywhere besides ovals and training grounds. Beaches in summer, of course—swimming and running on the sand were part of the family's fitness regimen.

As she'd strolled past modern or renovated buildings a window display advertising Barossa Valley wine triggered a light-bulb moment. The Valley, the Fleurieu Peninsula and the Adelaide Hills, plus many other tourist areas, were all within easy driving distance, and she'd been promised a two-week vacation as soon as the assignment ended. All she'd need were a map, a plan and a hire car.

She picked up Chinese takeaway, and spent the evening poring over brochures and making notes. In full view from her window a group of young athletes were training in the parklands over the road. On the side-lines some adults watched and encouraged. Others sat on the grass with younger children, playing games or reading with them.

Her eyes were drawn to a man sitting with a boy on his lap, their heads bent as small fingers traced words or pictures in a book. Her chest tightened and she crossed her arms in a self-hug. Why didn't she have any memories of those occasions? Why had she never asked either parent to read to her or share a favourite television show with her? She'd always been too afraid of rejection.

Why had *they* never noticed her quietly waiting for some of the attention claimed by her boisterous brothers? If it had been intentional maybe it wouldn't hurt so much. Being overlooked cut deeper than deliberately being ignored. And she'd never been able to summon up the courage to intentionally draw attention to herself.

The boy looked up, talking with animation to his father. Eyes locked, they were in a world of their own.

It conjured up the image of Matt Dalton holding her gaze captive as they'd talked. Even thinking of those weary blue eyes spiked her pulse, and memories of that long-ago kiss resurfaced. Her balcony secret she'd never revealed to anyone. Never intended to.

Lauren chose a different route to work in the morning. She felt more herself, determined to show her new boss she was the professional his friend had recommended.

Last night no matter how many positions she'd tried or how often she'd thumped the pillows, sleep had eluded her. Reruns of her two encounters with Matt Dalton had kept her awake until she'd given in, got up, and researched the company. Something she normally avoided to keep distance and objectivity.

There'd been no reference to him, only a Marcus Dalton who'd become successful by investing in small businesses, and persuading others to participate too. The website hadn't been updated since November last year, indicating there'd been difficulties around that time.

No, wait. She'd been asked to assess twenty-one months. So the anomalies had been discovered only recently but long-term deception was suspected.

The sleep she'd eventually managed had been deep and dreamless, surprising since her last thoughts and first on awakening had been of full grim lips and jaded midnight-blue eyes.

* * *

The door adjacent to Mr Dalton's was still locked. From the piles of folders on his desk and extension, he'd arrived very early. He appeared even wearier, the shadows under his eyes even darker.

Lauren tried to ignore the quick tug low in her abdomen, and the quickening of her pulse.

'Good morning, Mr Dalton. Would it be possible to have the outer door unlocked so I won't disturb you going in and out?'

Or be disturbed by my immature reaction to you.

Intense blue eyes scanned her face, reigniting the warm glow from yesterday.

'Good morning, Ms Taylor. I'm not easily disturbed.'

Of course you're not. You're a cause not a recipient. Ignite a girl's senses with a soul-shattering kiss then forget her. Though to be fair she'd been the one to run.

'My watch alarm is set for an hourly reminder to relieve my eyes, stretch and drink water. To ease my back, I sometimes walk around or up and down a few flights of stairs.'

'Not a problem.' He glanced at the bottle in her hand. 'Keep anything you like in the fridge under the coffee machine or there's a larger one in the staffroom.'

Without looking, he flicked a hand towards a door in the wall behind him. 'There's an ensuite bathroom here or, if you prefer, washrooms on the far side of Reception.'

Why the flash of anguish in his eyes? Why was she super alert, her skin tingling during this mundane conversation?

'Thank you.' She turned towards the bench, away from his probing gaze, popped her drink bottle and morning snack into the fridge, then went to her desk. Keeping her eyes averted didn't prevent his masculine aroma teasing her nostrils as she passed him.

She settled at her new station and, while the system booted up, filled in the personnel document he'd left for her. Once everything was laid in her preferred setting, she stood by the window to stare at the distant hills for a slow count of fifteen.

Now she was ready to start.

For two hours, apart from a short break for her eyes, she focused on the screens in front of her. But like a radio subliminally intruding into your dreams, some part of her was acutely aware of each time the man next door spoke on the phone or accessed the filing cabinets in this room.

The feeling in the pit of her stomach now was different, familiar, one she found comfortable, the exhilaration of the chase. The minor errors matched those in the audits. The one anomaly she found was puzzling enough for her to recheck from the beginning, puzzling enough to tease her brain.

A challenge worthy of the fee her boss charged Dalton Corporation.

She headed for the ensuite to freshen up ready for coffee, cheese crackers and relief time. There was one door on her left, another along the corridor to her right.

She regretted choosing the latter the moment she saw the iron-smooth black and silver patterned quilt covering a king-sized bed. For a nanosecond she pictured rumpled sheets half covering a bare-chested Matt, his features composed in tranquil sleep. She blinked and pivoted round. Not an image she wanted in her head when she locked eyes with this cheerless, work-driven man.

On her return to the office, his posture enforced her last description. His chin rested on his hands, his elbows on the desk, his attention fully absorbed by the text on his screen.

Stealing the opportunity to observe him unnoticed, she stopped. A perception of unleashed power bunched in his shoulders, a dogged single-mindedness showed in his concentration. The untrimmed ends of his thick hair brushed the collar of his shirt, out of character to her perception of a smart, city businessman.

His mug had been pushed to the edge of his desk, presumably empty. She picked it up, startling him.

'Would you like a refill?'

He nodded. 'Thanks. Flat white from the machine, one sugar. How's it going?'

'Progressing. Do you want details?'

His eyes narrowed.

She pre-empted his next remark. 'People who hire me have varying knowledge of technology and require different levels of explanation.' *Many don't like to betray their ignorance in the field.* 'My daily report will be comprehensive.'

'Do whatever's necessary to get results. I'll read the report.' Again an undertone of irritation further roughened his voice, a darkening glint of angst flashed in his eyes.

Matt made a note in red at the top of the paper in front of him, and regretted being repeatedly terse with her. He closed his eyes, clasped his neck, and arched his back. He felt bone tired from sitting, reading, and trying to make sense of his father's recent actions.

He wished he could shake the guilt for not being around, for not noticing the subtle changes on his trips home for family occasions. Maybe if he'd spent more one-on-one time with Marcus he would have. Instead he'd apportioned blame without considering it was their lives, their marriage. For nine years he'd kept physical and emotional distance from two of the most important people in his life.

He heard the soft clunk of a mug on wood. By the time he straightened and looked, a steaming coffee sat within reach, and Lauren was disappearing into her room. She'd discarded the light jacket she'd worn on arrival. Tired as he was, the male in him appreciated her slender figure, her trim waist. The pertness of her bottom in the grey trousers.

Inappropriate. Unprofessional.

As he drank the strong brew the sound of a quirky ringtone spun his head. The friendliness of Lauren's greeting to someone called Pete rankled for no reason. Her musical laughter ignited a heat wave along his bloodstream.

He strode to the ensuite to splash water on his face and cool down.

'Hey, it's nearly twelve o'clock.'

Lauren started, jerking round to see her temporary boss standing in the doorway, the remoteness in his eyes raising goosebumps on her skin. She blinked and checked her watch.

'Two minutes to go. Are you keeping tabs on my schedule?' Some clients did.

'Not specifically.' He moved further into the room, closer to her desk. To her.

Her pulse had no right to rev up. Her lungs had no right to expand, seeking his masculine aroma.

'Your work's high intensity.' His neutral tone brought her to earth.

'I've learnt how to manage it. Results take patience and time.'

He gave a masculine grunt followed by a wry grin. 'The latter's not something we have plenty of. Take a lunch break. I need you fully alert.'

Eight floors by foot before taking the elevator to the ground helped keep her fit. She smiled and walked out into the light drizzle. Adelaide was like a new city waiting to be explored. Chomping on a fresh salad roll, she strolled along, musing on that dour man, wondering what, or who, had caused the current situation. And why Marcus Dalton was no longer in charge.

Matt was clearly related. He bore a strong resemblance to the photograph on the website she'd accessed. Even with the ravages of the trauma he was under, he was incredibly handsome with an innate irresistible charisma. Was he married? In a relationship?

She chastised herself, chanting silently, *Never let anyone get to you on assignments*. Stupid and unprofessional, it could only lead to complications and tears. However, she had never been in this situation before…she'd never been kissed by one of her clients.

'There's definitely a recurrent anomaly. Finding when it started may tell me how and what,' Lauren informed Matt as she gave him her report prior to going home.

She was leaning towards it being deliberate because of the number of identical anomalies. No reason to mention she had no idea how it had been achieved.

He nodded and dropped the report in a tray.

'How's the hotel? I asked Joanne to book some-where not too far out.'

'Oh.' Was he trying to be sociable? Make amends for his abruptness? 'Very nice, and my room overlooks the parklands.'

'Not too noisy on that corner?'

She couldn't suppress her grin. 'I live in Sydney, remember. You tune it out or drown it with music.'

His gaze held hers for an eon, or longer. The darkening in the midnight-blue coincided with heat tendrils coiling through her from a fiery core low in her abdomen. Her eyes refused to break contact, her mouth refused to say goodbye. Her muscles refused to obey the command to turn her away.

It was Matt who broke the spell, flinching away and shaking his head. His chest heaved as his lungs fought for air. He clenched his fists to curb the impulse to—no, he wouldn't even think it.

'Did you bus or taxi?' He didn't particularly care but was desperate to keep the conversation normal. To ignore those golden specks making her eyes shine like the gemstones in his mother's extensive jewellery collection. His voice sounded as if he'd sprinted the last metres of a marathon.

'I walked. It's not that far.'

His eyebrows shot up. 'Walked?' To and from a bus stop or taxi rank was the furthest most women he knew went on foot, apart from in shopping centres.

She shrugged. 'Beats paying gym fees and clears my head.'

'I guess. Just take care, okay.' He had no reason to worry, yet he did.

'Always. Good afternoon, Mr Dalton.'

'I'll see you tomorrow, Ms Taylor.'

As soon as she'd gone he slumped in his chair, stunned by his reaction to her smile, quick and genuine, lighting up her face. His pulse had hiked up, his chest tightened. And his body had responded quicker and stronger than ever before.

His fingers gripped the armrests as he fought for control. This shouldn't, couldn't be happening. Women, *all* women were out of bounds at the moment. Even for no-strings, no-repercussions sex. She was here on a temporary basis. She was an employee, albeit once removed.

He groaned. She was temptation.

He forced his mind to conjure up visions of the life he'd left behind in London, crowded buses and packed Tubes, nightclubs, cafés and old pubs. Teeming, exciting. Energising. Attractive, fashionably dressed women in abundance. Great job, great friends. And one woman he'd thought he'd truly known.

It had been a near perfect world prior to his trust going down the gurgler and his existence being uprooted into chaos. Now he had little social life, even less free time, and collapsed wearily into a deep dreamless sleep every night. And woke early each morning to the same hectic scenario.

CHAPTER THREE

MATT WAS PACING the floor, talking on the phone when Lauren arrived Thursday morning, hoping for a repeat of yesterday when she'd been left pretty much alone all day. He'd been absent when she'd finished so she'd left her report on his desk.

On the way to her room she returned the preoccupied nod he gave her, grinning to herself at the double take he gave her suitcase and overnight bag. She'd booked out of the hotel, confirmed she'd be returning on Monday and been promised the same room.

She did her routine and began work, fully expecting an apologetic call some time from her eldest brother, who'd been delegated to pick her up on arrival in Melbourne. She'd long ago accepted she was way down on her family's priority list.

Her priority was to complete her designated task. Her expertise told her a human hand was involved. If—*when, Lauren, think positive*—she solved what and how, fronting Matt Dalton was going to be daunting. The few occasions she'd had to implicate someone in a position of trust had always left her feeling queasy, as if she were somehow to blame.

In two days she'd become used to the sound

of him in the background like a soft radio music channel where the modulations and nuances were subtle, never intrusive. Every so often the complete silence told her he'd left the office. Occasionally someone came in. Few stayed more than a couple of minutes.

There was no sign of him when she went to the fridge, though an unrolled diagram lay spread out on his desk. She resisted the impulse to take a peek, and consumed her snack while enjoying the view from her window.

Matt's return was preceded by his voice as he walked along the corridor not long after she resumed work. She glimpsed him as he strode past her doorway to the window, ramrod-straight, hand clenched. Not a happy man.

His temper wouldn't improve when her report showed all she'd written down so far today was a slowly growing number of random dates.

'Dad!'

His startled tone broke Lauren's concentration.

'Sorry, mate, I'll call you back. *Dad*, what are you doing here?'

He came into her view and stopped. By craning her neck, she could see him clasping a greying man to his chest.

'You came alone?' There was genuine concern in his tone.

'Haven't been in for weeks so I thought I'd come and find out what's happening.' Apart from the

slower pace of the words, the voice's similarity to
Matt's was defining.

'Everything's going smoothly. Come and sit
down. We'll talk over coffee.'

Blocking his father's view of her, he guided him
towards the seating, then continued talking as he
passed her door on the way to make the drinks.
Without breaking step he made a quick gesture
across his throat when their eyes met.

'There's a new espresso flavour you've never
tried, rich and aromatic.'

He wanted her to shut down and not let his father
know what she was doing. What if Marcus came
in here? Asked who she was? As far as she knew,
it was still his company. And it was his son's fault
she couldn't escape through the locked door.

The papers and folder were slipped into the
drawer, a fresh page on the pad partially covered
by random notes for show. Acutely conscious of the
mingled sounds of the coffee machine and Matt's
muted voice making a call, she reached for the
mouse.

Matt slid his mobile into his pocket, and picked
up the two small cups. What the hell had prompted
his father's arrival? If his mother was aware he'd
come into the city, she'd be worried sick. Had Ms
Taylor understood his silent message? Could things
get any worse?

'Here, Dad, try this. Tell me if you like it.' He
sank into the other armchair, torn between the de-

sire to hug his ailing father, and the recurring craving to demand why he'd cheated on his wife. So many times.

He'd never understood why so many people he knew treated cheating casually, as part of modern life. To him it was abhorrent. Why claim to love someone and then seek another partner? Why stay with someone who had no respect for your affection?

He had never declared the emotion, deeming that would be hypocritical, but had always insisted on fidelity. He'd found out the hard way that for some people promises meant nothing.

It churned Matt's stomach that his father considered affairs a normal part of life, his due entitlement as a charismatic male. The man he'd revered in his youth and aspired to become had seen no reason why they should affect his marriage.

He was torn between the deep love of a son for his father and distaste for his casual attitude to being faithful. And behind him, hidden by the wall in Matt's eye line, was the room where he brought the women. His coffee turned sour in his mouth.

Marcus sipped his drink cautiously, savouring the taste.

'Mmm…good, real coffee. I'll take a pod home and ask Rosalind to buy some.'

'Take a box.' Matt cleared his throat, hesitant to ask the vital question. *Please don't let the answer be he drove.* 'How did you get here, Dad?'

'Caught a cab at the shopping centre near home.' He glared at the desk, set not too far away. 'You've twisted my desk.' It was an accusation.

'Don't worry, it suits *me* that way. We can always put it back.' He'd never place it in the former position that had given the user a direct eye line to the person working at the desk next door.

'Hmph. Now I need the bathroom.'

Marcus put his cup on the table, and went to the ensuite. Matt let out a long huff of breath, and took another drink of the hot, stimulating liquid. A glance at his watch told him his cousin should be here in a few minutes.

Swearing softly when his desk phone rang, he strode over to answer. He missed his father's return as he searched his in-tray for the letter the caller had sent.

Lauren stopped typing as Marcus came into her office. The eyes were a similar colour, the facial features bore a strong resemblance, but he lacked the firm line of his son's jaw, his innate sense of character.

'You're new. What happened to Miss…?' He tapped his palm on his forehead. 'Um, long dark hair, big blue eyes.'

'I believe she left. Can I help you?'

His gaze intensified, then he came round to stand beside her, and stared at the screen.

'She was a good typist. Fast and accurate.'

'Dad.'

Matt stood in the doorway, the same forbidding expression he'd worn at her interview directed at her. She lifted her chin, determined not to be part of whatever games this family was playing.

The older man spoke first. 'There's too many changes, Matthew. My girl was good. She left. People kept leaving.' Slow with pauses at inappropriate times. 'Who hired this one?'

He tapped her on the shoulder as he spoke, and she involuntarily flinched, knew from the frown on Matt's face he'd seen. He came over, and wrapped his arm across his father's shoulders.

'Let's leave Ms Taylor to her work, Dad. Come and finish your coffee?'

Although Matt barely glanced at her screen, he gave her a reassuring nod as he led his father out. He'd seen the bogus letter she'd started typing up.

'It'll be cold.'

She heard the outer door open, and saw Matt's body sag in relief.

'Here's Alan, Dad. He and I will drive you home and Mum will brew you another when we arrive.'

They moved out of her sight and she heard muffled exchanges then Matt's clearer words.

'Give me a minute. Grab that box of pods from the bench.'

He came into her room, his grateful expression telling her she'd pleased him, creating fissions of pleasure skittling from cell to cell.

'Quick thinking, Ms Taylor, thank you. I'll be

gone for an hour or so. Joanne has a key to lock my office if you go out.'

He paused, swallowed as if there was more he wanted to say but couldn't find the words, then disappeared leaving her with a bundle of questions she'd never be game to ask.

The man she'd just met hadn't looked all that old but his behaviour and actions were certainly not those of a fast-thinking entrepreneur who'd built a thriving business.

She deleted the text as soon as she heard the door close, and brought up the files she'd been scanning. The events replayed in her mind as she sat, hands lightly resting on the keyboard.

Matt had been protective yet somehow detached from his father, desperate to get him out of here. He'd called this Alan to come and help, not wanting to escort him alone.

From Marcus' remark she deduced Matt had taken over his office. A woman had worked in here so he'd been elsewhere, probably the empty room by reception. Had Marcus kept such tight control Matt had no idea what was happening in the accounts and records?

That would explain his underlying antipathy and hostile manner but why towards her? She was his solution, his last resort. She was used to being warmly welcomed and treated with respect.

Matt was an enigma, his words and tone not always matching his body language and often conflicting with the message in those stunning blue eyes. He resented whatever it was that sparked between them, and must have a reason she couldn't fathom.

At all costs she had to find and fix his problems and get away without him finding out they had a past.

Matt quietly placed his keys into his desk drawer, wondering what he was going to say to Lauren.

My father has Alzheimer's. He's losing his memory. He's lost most of his good staff in the last year, and he's possibly screwed up the company.

His condition had escalated in the last month and Matt's mother was finding it harder to cope. Some very tough decisions would have to be made in the near future.

Matt would never blame Marcus for anything that could be attributed to that hellish affliction. But it was his father's screwing around that had sent him to the other side of the world. If he'd been here, possibly working with him, he'd have noticed the deterioration in time to prevent this debacle.

He would have. His fingers bunched. He squeezed his eyes shut and gritted his teeth. *He would have.*

Only the family, their doctor and a few select friends knew. Matt believed his chances of success hinged on keeping it a secret, and Lauren's

employer had emphasised her discretion and trust-
worthiness. He was about to test it to the max.

She stopped working as he came to her doorway, her face inscrutable, her eyes wary. His stomach clenched.

'We'd better talk. Please come in here.'

Once they were seated by the window he paused
to think, weighing up how much to tell her.

'There aren't the words to thank you enough for
your understanding today. The man you saw isn't
the same person who started this company. He has
Alzheimer's.'

She leant forward. 'I suspected something like
that. I'm sorry. It must be so hard on your family.'
Empathy rang true in her voice and showed in her
expression.

'Unfortunately, he kept his illness a secret from
everyone, including my mother. We have no idea
how long he faked his way until the progression
sped up and his errors in the business became obvious. I'd have come home sooner if I'd known.'

'You weren't here?' She recoiled, eyes big and
bright, fingers splayed.

She didn't know? There'd been no reason to tell
her but he'd assumed she'd guessed. He nodded.
'I've been living in England for seven years.'

'Oh. Did you ever work here with your father?'

'In my late teens. My interests are in different
fields of business.'

A pink blush spread up her neck and cheeks.

'Is something wrong?' He tensed, flexed his shoulders, and his hand lifted in concern.

Lauren cursed her lifelong affliction. What *could* possibly be wrong?

Only that the instant he mentioned his teens she remembered the balcony. Only that the sight of his mouth forming the words had her lips recalling the gentle touch of his.

'No, and I promise never to divulge any personal or company information to anyone.' Her hands clasped in her lap, she could barely take in that he'd shared this most personal secret with her. Now she understood.

His unplanned return from abroad to take control of a company in financial trouble explained the tension, the curtness. The urgency. She couldn't begin to imagine the daunting task he'd had thrust upon him.

'I'd appreciate it.'

'You're welcome. That's why you wanted my scanning hidden from him and called a friend for help.'

'He has good and bad days. Normally he becomes agitated whenever anything to do with the company is mentioned yet today he gave the taxi driver the correct address for the office. There was no hesitation in finding his way here or to the en-suite.'

'And he remembered the girl who worked here, though not her name.'

'He would.' The bitterness in his voice shook her and she jerked back, receiving a half-smile in apology as he continued.

'I was told her departure a few months ago was acrimonious to say the least. There were others who left because of his behaviour too, but replacements have to wait until you succeed and we sort everything out.'

She'd go and new staff would come. There'd be another woman at her desk, chosen by him…what was she thinking? This was not a valid reason to be depressed. Did he prefer blondes or brunettes?

Must. Stop. Thinking like this.

She snapped herself out of it and went to stand. 'On that note, I'd better get back to my task.'

He stood, and held out his hand to help her. The warmth from his touch spread up her arm, radiating to every part of her. She doubted even ice-cold water would cool her down. She prayed he couldn't detect her tremor and didn't demur as he kept hold.

'I am truly grateful, Lauren. I owe you big time and I never forget a debt.'

The message in his smouldering dark blue eyes painted a graphic picture of the form his gratitude might take, scrambling every coherent thought in her brain. Her throat dried, butterflies stirred in her stomach and it felt as if fluttering wings were brushing against every cell on her skin.

His grip tightened. Her lips parted. He leant closer.

The phone on his desk shattered the moment, and he glowered at it as he moved back, and reluctantly released her. She caught the arm of the chair to avoid collapsing into it.

His rasping, 'We'll talk again later,' proved she wasn't the only one affected.

As he picked up the handset he added, 'Alan's my cousin, family.'

The instant he answered the call he was in corporate mode. That irked because she needed time to compose herself, cool her skin, but he clearly didn't. When she returned from the ensuite, he was leaning on his desk, phone to his ear, watching for her. His engaging smile and quick but thorough appraisal from her face to her feet and back threatened to undo her freshen up. Not so calm and composed after all, just better at covering it up.

Lauren closed down early, allowing time for the ride to the airport, loath to suspend her search for four days. She had an inkling of an idea she'd heard somewhere but couldn't remember where or when. There'd be plenty of time to dwell on it in Melbourne.

Collecting her luggage, she took her report to Matt, whose stunned face and glance at his watch proved he'd forgotten her early departure.

'That late already? Have you ordered a taxi?'

'I'll be fine. I've noticed they always seem to be driving past.'

He grinned. 'Unless you need one. I'll finish this page and drive you.'

'There's no—'

'Humour me.'

Lauren's knowledge of cars was limited—there wasn't a necessity to own one in Sydney—but she recognised the Holden emblem on the grill. Matt's quiet assurance as he eased into the traffic didn't surprise her.

'Did you drive in Europe?'

'Yes, rarely in London, a lot through the country. Nowhere is too far if you can put up with dense traffic and miles of freeways. So different from Australia. Driving in Paris was a unique experience. Have you travelled?'

'A week in Bali with friends two years ago. We're planning a trip for this year if we can decide on a destination.'

She was aware of him glancing at her, but she kept her focus on the road where his should be.

'You mentioned family in Melbourne. Do you visit often?'

'Three or four times a year. This is my niece's first Easter.'

Matt willed her to look his way. She didn't. The ten-to-fifteen-minute drive in heavy traffic was hardly conducive to a meaningful discussion. That would have to wait until she returned.

'Why did you move to Sydney?' Why did he

want to know? Why the long silent pause as she considered his question?

'Why did you go to London?'

Because I couldn't stand the sight of my parents feigning a happy marriage when it was a complete sham.

Because even moving into a rented house with friends in another suburb hadn't given him sufficient distance.

'Rite of passage to fly the nest and try to climb the corporate ladder without favour from associates of my father.'

'And you succeeded. It'll all be waiting for you when you've got Dalton Corporation back on track. Your family must be glad to have you home even under sad circumstances. I'm sure they've missed you.'

Matt picked up on the nuance in her voice, but didn't respond as he flicked on his indicator and turned into the airport road. So she had an issue with family as well. She'd rather not go.

He pulled into a clear space at the drop-off zone and switched off the engine. Before he had a chance to walk round and assist her, Lauren had unlatched her seat belt and jumped out.

He wiped his hand across his jaw, fighting the urge to reassure her, feeling he'd left so much unsaid today. He'd make time when she came back. She *was* coming back, and that pleased him.

She let him lift her luggage from the boot, and seemed reluctant to say goodbye.

'Thank you for the lift, Mr Dalton. I'll see you on Tuesday.'

'My pleasure. Enjoy your long weekend.'

I don't understand why, but I'll miss you.

CHAPTER FOUR

DRIVING BACK, MATT felt like laughing out loud at the incongruity of the situation. They could have spent time together during the four-day break, working alone, sharing lunches, maybe even dinner. Learning more about each other. Instead they'd be in different states paying lip service to family traditions.

With a complete turnaround, he wondered what the hell he was thinking. This was insane. Lauren Taylor was a temporary employee. Not his type at all. Yet he'd been so close to kissing her today in the office. The action and location were both bad ideas. So why did he wish that call hadn't come at that moment?

And how the hell had she managed to avoid answering his question?

Lauren closed her novel, and stared at the landscape rushing by then disappearing as the plane gained height. How could she concentrate on spine-thrilling action when her mind was in turmoil because of a man? She had male friends, a few of them treasured and platonic with whom she felt completely comfortable and totally at ease.

There were none who made her forget to breathe,

who created fire in her core and sent her pulse into an erratic drumbeat. The thought of the magic those now skilful lips might evoke had her quivering with anticipation, earning her an anxious mutter from the older woman in the adjacent seat.

She gave her a reassuring smile, and turned back to the window. The fantasies she'd concocted for the last ten years had been childish daydreams based on teenage romance. The two relationships she'd drifted into had been more from affable proximity than passion. That they'd remained friends to this day proved how little anyone's heart had been involved.

No way would any woman accept friendship after an affair with Matt Dalton. His touch created electrical fissions on her skin, turned her veins into a racecourse and curled her toes. If they ever made it to the bedroom… She gulped in air, imagining the tanned, hot muscles he hid under expensive executive shirts.

'Are you sure you're okay?'

Her head swung round to meet a concerned gaze.

'Yes, thank you. I'm fine.'

Opening her book, she pretended to read, flipped pages and didn't take in a solitary word.

Late on Saturday night Lauren curled into the pillows in the guest bedroom, wondering what Matt was doing. She almost wished she'd gone with her parents and the grandchildren to visit friends. Her brothers were having the inevitable barbecue in the back garden.

She'd spent a great day with friends from university, who had insisted on driving her home, dropping her off at the corner because of all the cars parked in the street. Deciding to try to be more sociable, she'd attempted to join in with her brothers' party.

She'd lasted ten minutes among the raucous crowd, with whom she had little in common, then she'd finished her sausage sandwich, drained the soft drink can and said goodnight. A chorus of, 'Night, little sister!' had followed her into the house, most of it slurred.

She'd gone slowly up the stairs, reappraising her attitude to her upbringing. Had she been the one to pull away, uneasy with the openness of the rest of her family? Had she taken their leave-her-in-peace approach for indifference?

Not understanding why she'd begun to analyse her relationships, she'd shaken it away. She had a good life, a great job and supportive friends. Maybe she'd talk it through with them when she went home.

Putting on headphones and turning her music up loud, she'd logged into her computer and accessed her favourite game, which necessitated super concentration, blocking everything else out.

Now it was quiet except for an occasional passing vehicle. Was Matt asleep? Did he live alone or with his parents? Did he have siblings? There were so many questions that might never be answered.

Matt laughed out loud as he stood chest-high in his parents' pool on Sunday afternoon, pretending to fight off his nephews. He picked up Drew, the youngest, and tossed him, squirming and shrieking, about a metre away. Alex immediately latched onto his upper arm.

'Me next, Uncle Matt. Me next.'

He obliged, knowing this game could last until they were exhausted. He was surprised they had so much energy after the active Easter egg hunt around the garden this morning. One after the other, they kept coming at him and he revelled in their joy of the simple pleasure. They rejuvenated him whenever he was with them.

These were the times he regretted never marrying, and having children of his own. He took a splash of water in the face, shook his head, and laughed again. Hell, he wasn't even thirty, he had plenty of time.

He grabbed them both, one in each arm. Knowing what was coming, they giggled and clung to his neck. 'Deep breath.' Taking one himself, he dropped to the bottom of the pool, bending his legs to give him leverage. Pushing up, he surged from the water in a great spray, their happy squeals deafening him.

'Again. Again.

'Time out.'

His sister, Lena, was walking across the lawn carrying a tray of drinks and snacks. He let the boys go and they immediately swam for the ladder. Hoisting himself up onto the side, he took the beer she offered. She sat beside him, letting her feet dangle into the water, and studied him as he drank.

'What?' He looked at her and grinned. 'Am I in trouble?'

She shook her head as her eyes roamed over his face, and rested a caring hand on his arm. 'There's something different about you, Matt. I can't quite work out what.'

'I'm bone-tired, grabbing fast food most days and need a haircut.'

And I am inexplicably missing a woman I have only known for three days.

'Nothing's changed there since I last saw you. Bigger problems at work? No, that you'd handle in your usual indomitable manner.'

She tilted her head and arched her eyebrows, a ploy that usually produced a confession. They were as close as siblings could get but Lauren was new and he hadn't quite worked out how and why she affected him. And what he was going to do about it.

'Every trip you made home I hoped you'd have found peace from whatever drove you to go so far away. It never happened though you hid it well, and I know you only came now because Dad needed you.'

He didn't reply because he couldn't explain. He shrugged, put his arm around her and drew her close.

'I missed you, Mark and the boys more than I can say, Lena. You're the biggest plus on the side of me staying for good.'

Her face lit up at his remark he was considering relocating back to Adelaide. He meant it, wanted to be here for all his nephews' milestones. Skype was no substitute for personal hugs.

She kissed his cheek. 'You'll tell me when you're ready. In the meantime, add an extra plus sign.'

He frowned then grinned even wider and bear-hugged her. 'That's great. When?'

'November. You're the first to know.'

'Whatever happens I'll be here.' It was a promise he intended to keep.

When the boys went inside with their mother, he slid back into the water, working off restless energy with strong freestyle laps. His strokes and turns were automatic, leaving his mind to wonder what Lauren was doing and who she was with. And why the hell it was beginning to matter to him.

'Hang on, Lauren. The door's locked.'

Lauren turned her head towards the sound. It was ten past seven on Tuesday morning. Where was Matt? He'd said nothing about being absent today.

Joanne appeared, carrying a small bunch of keys, and they walked along the corridor.

'Mr Dalton's at a site meeting in the northern suburbs, called me last night. If he's not back by morning break, I'll join you for coffee.' She pushed the door open and left.

Being alone in the office didn't daunt Lauren, who'd always preferred having no surrounding noise or motion. Today her body was all keyed up as if waiting for some fundamental essential that was missing.

She had no interruptions until ten-thirty when Joanne walked in carrying a plate of home-baked jam slices.

'Family favourite. Let's sit by the window. Tea or coffee?'

'Tea, thanks.'

Lauren never indulged in gossip at work. She couldn't define why she felt tempted now, unless it was because Matt Dalton had invaded her peace of mind, and aroused her curiosity. The more she learnt about him, the easier it might be to resist him. If she couldn't she knew who'd end up heartbroken.

'How long have you worked for the Daltons?'

'Over six years. Since my youngest started secondary school. Of course, that was in a smaller office near the parklands. I like having familiar faces around. How do you cope, travelling and working with new people all the time?'

'I prefer it. I'm not much of a people person, never quite got the hang of casual socialising.'

'Mr Dalton senior was a natural and had no problems persuading people to invest with him. He was good with computers, installing quite a few new programs himself, and very easy to work for until a few years ago. We lost good long-term staff because he became secretive and less approachable.'

'And now Matt's in charge.'

Of everything. Thankfully he was unaware that included her emotions, unaware of how intriguing she found him.

'He came back from Europe when his father's heart trouble was diagnosed. Put a great career on hold, I understand, and not very happy to be here. I'm not sure whether it's the business, the problems or having to leave London, maybe all of them. He'll be heading back once his father's in full health again.'

Lauren let her babble on, regretting she'd instigated the topic. Matt had led her to believe he trusted Joanne yet he'd given the staff a fabricated story and let them believe his father would be coming back.

Did he really think any of them were involved in the computer anomalies? If not, it was cruel of him to give them false hope. Why did he keep giving out mixed messages? Or was she misinterpreting them?

Oh, why wasn't he older, content with a doting wife, and heading for a paunch from all her home cooking?

Lauren's mobile rang as she wrote notes on the last hour's work. Convincing Matt of her beliefs wasn't going to be an easy task.

'Ms Taylor, I need a favour.'

No preamble. No 'how are things going?' And the rasping tone was rougher. Why did she sympathise with his stress when he obviously intended to unload some of it onto her?

'Yes, Mr Dalton.'

'This is taking longer than I anticipated. If a Duncan Ford arrives at the office while I'm out, can you entertain him until I arrive?'

'Me?'

Meet and socialise with an unknown corporate executive?

Dealing with them when they needed her skills and the conversation centred on their technical problems was a world away from casual chit-chat. Knowing she was capable gave her confidence.

'You. Will it be a problem? Joanne's compiling figures for our meeting later.' He sounded irritated at her reluctance.

'That's not what I do. The few businessmen I've met have only been interested in how quickly I can fix their problems. A comment about the weather is as personal as we'd get.'

'It won't be for long. I'll be there in an hour or so, depending on traffic.'

She heard another voice in the background, followed by his muttered reply.

'Please, Ms Taylor. He's just a man.'

Yeah, like you're *just a man.*

His coaxing tone teased goose bumps to rise on her skin, and the butterflies in her stomach to take flight. She'd do it for him, and he knew it. She could hardly tell him fear of messing it up for him contributed to her reticence.

'Give him coffee. Ask him about the weekend football or his grandkids. Pretend he's an android.'

She pictured him grinning as he said that, and sighed.

'Okay, I'll try.'

After an abrupt 'thanks' he hung up, leaving her with a sinking stomach and a strong craving for chocolate, *her* standby for stress. Grabbing her bag, she raced for the lift and the café in the next building, mentally plotting dire consequences for all the too-good-looking, excessively privileged, overly confident males who'd ever tried to manipulate her. Including her three brothers.

'Mr Ford has arrived, Lauren. I'll bring him along.' Joanne phoned to give her warning.

Shoot. Only ten minutes since Matt called to

say he was finally on his way. She swallowed a mouthful of water, pulled her shoulders back and prayed she didn't look as apprehensive as she felt. On her way through his office she added an extra plea he had a clear traffic run.

Mr Ford was average height, slightly overweight, and wore an apologetic smile. So much for Matt's word picture. He also held a small boy by the hand.

'Ms Taylor? Thank you for offering to look after us until Matt gets here.'

Offering? Us? Someone tall and desperate had bent the truth a tad.

'You're welcome. Come on in.' She indicated towards the armchairs. 'Please take a seat. Would—?'

Squealing with excitement, the child had broken free and was running to the window.

'Look, Granddad. Look how high we are. Look at the tiny cars way down there.'

Granddad smiled at Lauren and shrugged. 'The world's a wondrous place at that age.'

He walked over and hunkered down, his arm around the boy's shoulders, and let the child point out the amazing things he could see.

Pain clamped round Lauren's heart and she couldn't bear to watch them. She clasped her hands together over her stomach and stared at the floor. She'd never shared a special moment like this with either of her parents. They'd been happy to supply her with books, computers and assorted accessories, hoping they would keep her occupied. Never seemed to have time to spend exclusively with her.

There'd never been other relatives either. Her father's family lived in Canada, her mother had left home in her teens, and contact was limited on both sides. No wonder she felt inept in any new social situation.

'I believe you were about to offer coffee, Ms Taylor.'

She looked up to meet a quizzical gaze. Knew she was being appraised and managed a shaky smile. Matt had requested her to hostess and he was paying her wage, so a hostess she'd try to be.

'Of course. We have water or soft drinks if the child is thirsty.'

And then what do I talk to you about?

Take out the economy, sport, politics and local events, none of which she was up with, and she was left with the weather.

Matt Dalton, I hate you for putting me in this position.

He'd hired her to sit and scan his computer files, not make small talk, which she'd never ever been able to comprehend.

'Flat white for me and lemonade for Ken, thank you. I came in to take care of him while my wife and daughter saw a specialist, took a punt that Matt might be free. Ken has a game pad, and I have a magazine to read so we won't be a bother.'

He reached for the satchel he'd placed on the floor and opened it.

It's no trouble,' she lied.

His expression said he didn't believe her, and knew exactly how she was feeling. He'd be a formidable opponent in a boardroom. She turned away, heart hurting, stomach churning. Still the same tongue-tied girl she'd always been. Always would be.

Mr Ford was settled into a chair and Ken sitting cross-legged on the floor when she brought the drinks over. The boy was frowning as she put his on the low table.

'Thank you. Granddad, the frog won't jump.'

Without hesitation she dropped down alongside him.

'Show me.'

He studied her with narrowed eyes, assessing if she could be trusted with his new favourite toy. He gingerly handed it over, shuffled closer and didn't take his eyes off the screen as she read the game rules and started tapping.

Matt couldn't remember breaking a mirror or running over a black cat but he sure as hell was raking in bad luck. At least there'd been some positives in his inspection of a new recommended site today.

Duncan Ford was a man reputed to be fair and honest in business, a trustworthy partner and an admirable opponent. A man he'd met on a number of occasions over the years, usually with his father. Lately through a business acquaintance and his own initiative.

If Lauren had managed to keep him happy, he'd have a chance to pitch his proposition in the near future. If he secured a deal with Duncan Ford on the development of a vacant factory, it would go a long way to solving the company's present dilemma. Unfortunately ifs weren't solid happenings.

He strode towards his office, his heart sinking. No sound, no voices. Until, as he reached the open door, he heard a triumphant 'yes' in a child's tone.

The man he'd hoped to impress was sitting in one of the armchairs reading a magazine. Lauren and a young boy were kneeling by the coffee table, heads bent over a bright yellow pad.

'Matt.' Duncan stood, and came forward to shake hands. After putting the cardboard tube containing site plans on his desk and his satchel on the floor, Matt willingly complied.

'I apologise for not being here, Duncan.'

'Hey, it was an off chance. Lauren's been the perfect hostess.'

Matt flashed a grateful smile in her direction. He'd thank her properly later. The daggers she sent back warned him he'd have to grovel, big time. To his surprise he found the prospect stimulating rather than daunting.

'I got a call late yesterday to say this particular

site goes on the market next month. I couldn't re-fuse the chance to inspect it.'

'We'll schedule a meeting when you've finalised your proposal. My coming into town was unex-pected and I should be hearing from my daughter any minute. Once she and young Ken are on their way home, I'd like you and Lauren to join my wife and me for lunch.'

'Me?'

Matt's head swung at the panic in Lauren's voice. Exactly the same as earlier, yet, whatever her fears, she'd obviously impressed Duncan, which didn't surprise him. She certainly fascinated him.

'My treat for keeping Ken amused.'

'Thank you but no. I have work to do and I've brought my lunch.'

Her agitation was clear in her voice, and, though she managed to keep her features calm, Matt saw the plea in her wide-open eyes. And that intan-gible niggle flicked in his memory, and was gone just as fast.

The gentleman in him leaned towards letting her off the hook. The desperate male striving to secure a solid future for the company and its em-ployees won.

'It'll keep 'til tomorrow, Ms Taylor. Never re-fuse a chance to eat out in Adelaide.'

If she was about to protest, Ken forestalled her, patting her arm and holding up his pad.

'Your turn, Lauren.'

She knelt to attend to the child. The chagrined look she gave Matt ought to have annoyed him, as she'd be wined and dined in style. Instead he was already planning ways to help her relax with the Fords.

CHAPTER FIVE

CLAIR FORD AND her daughter were Lauren's idea of
true corporate wives, dressed in the latest fashion
and groomed to perfection. If their greetings and
appreciation hadn't been so sincere and friendly,
she might have cut and run.

With young mother and son safely on their way
home, the remaining four walked to the Fords' chosen restaurant. They led the way, allowing for private discussion.

'I owe you big time for today.' Matt's voice was
low and subdued, proving the tension he was under.

'I'll keep tally, Mr Dalton. This counts too. What
do I have in common with Mr Ford and his wife?
The nearest I come to their world is walking past
executive offices.'

'Under the current circumstances, Lauren, I
think you should call me Matt.'

Lauren. Matt.

This made it personal, more familiar.

She'd liked the way he'd remembered the pro-
nunciation of her name from her first phone call.
She wasn't so sure about the butterfly flutter in her
belly as he said it or the pleasurable shivers over
her skin every time he guided her past oncoming
pedestrians.

'I don't understand. You meet and deal with new people all the time. Why the reluctance?'

How could he understand how she felt? He oozed confidence and charm, would have no qualms on walking into a room full of notable people he'd never met. He'd been brought up to meet and greet strangers with ease.

'I can't do small talk. My family are all outgoing, garrulous, and at ease with anyone. I was shy. I'd freeze up and hide in my room. I...'

Duncan turned to check where they were as he and Clair turned off towards a waterside restaurant. The warm glow to her belly from Matt's gentle squeeze at her waist eased her misgivings. The tingles from his hot breath as he bent to her ear generated entirely different reservations.

'She's a down-to-earth mother and grandmother who enjoys serving on charity committees. He's into football and car racing. Trust me, Lauren, I'll be right beside you.'

They were escorted to a round table by the window. Matt held her chair, leaning over to whisper, 'Just be yourself, Lauren. I like you as you are.'

His fingers gently brushed a strand of hair from her shoulder, making her quiver, making her heart expand 'til her chest felt full and tight. So much for her internal lectures on the return flight to Adelaide, reinforcing how vital it was to keep distance between them.

Clair insisted on sitting next to her rather than

opposite. 'The men will talk shop,' she said without rancour, smiling as she accepted a menu. 'Always say they won't. Always do. Nature of the beast.'

At the moment the two of them were discussing wine with one waiter while another poured iced water into their glasses. Lauren drank some, and felt cooler, more in control.

'What do you fancy, Lauren? The veal scaloppini is always delicious, and the perfect size to leave room for dessert.' Clair put down her menu, her decision made.

After ordering the same, Lauren almost refused wine until she caught Matt watching her, and decided why not? It was a light refreshing Sauvignon Blanc and one glass might give her courage. It would also fortify her for later if she told him the most likely outcome.

'Duncan's a stickler for supporting local wineries and we're rarely disappointed,' Clair said, leaning closer. 'Ken really enjoyed himself today, told me you taught him how to win games faster.'

'He's very bright, picked up what I showed him easily.'

'Maybe I ought to get him to teach me. I'm hopeless. My worst fault is somehow sending files into folders they're not supposed to be in. Then I can't find them. I've also seized everything up a few times.'

'Have you taken any courses?' Chatting came naturally when someone took a genuine interest in you. Knowing they were all grateful to her, albeit for different reasons, helped too.

'A couple. I read the notes, and try to remember. Drives Duncan crazy. He says I rush too much. How do you do it all day?'

'Different people, different skills. Put me in a kitchen with any more than four or five ingredients, and I'm in trouble. Or rather, whoever wants to eat is.'

Their meals arrived, and the conversation became general until Clair suddenly announced, 'I'm thinking of asking Lauren to give me a lesson or two on my computer.'

Lauren saw a delighted smile replace the initial surprise on Matt's face. Duncan's exaggerated groan and loving expression towards his wife filled her with a longing she couldn't explain.

'I'm sure she's dealt with more incompetent people than me, Duncan Ford.' Clair's put-on piqued expression caused laughter round the table. Three pairs of eyes turned to Lauren for a reply.

'I'm sure I have. The trickiest ones are usually when they've tried to rectify the error but can't remember what they did. Or when they deny knowing.'

She shared a story of an ongoing promotion feud where two women had been sabotaging the other's computer, costing both of them their jobs. With encouragement she continued.

'A friend was asked to retrieve permanently deleted emails from the client's wife's laptop. He'd found romantic messages between her and another man, lost his temper and deleted them. Became angrier when he realised he now had nothing to confront her with.'

'Teach him to be destructive even *with* provocation. Did he get them back?' Clair asked.

'My friend refused to get involved so I have no idea.'

'Duncan, remember when…'

Clair's voice faded and Duncan's took over but Lauren barely heard his words. As she'd told the story, she'd become aware of Matt tensing beside her, hadn't dared look that way. She forced herself to focus on their host.

They were all laughing at the anecdote of his son-in-law wrongly directing an email about a surprise party when she glanced sideways. Matt was looking at her, a speculative expression on his face.

The world around them blurred until she could see only him. Her heart blipped then began to race. Warmth spread up her throat and cheeks. He arched his neck and his eyes darkened to almost black. She didn't dare guess at the thoughts behind them as he reached for his glass.

In fact Matt was wondering what the heck had happened. The quiet woman, who was so guarded with him, was captivating their hosts. There was only a hint of the hesitancy he'd perceived in the office. She listened to Clair with a genuine smile on her lips, and gave the same consideration to Duncan as he spoke.

So why the barrier with him? Instinct told him Lauren had a history with someone, painful enough to make her wary of men, or a particular breed of men. He was torn between letting it alone or finding out more and proving to her he couldn't be categorised.

It would be treading dangerous ground trying to discover the woman behind the technical façade. But, oh, it would feel good to see her smile focused on him, feel those sweet lips yield under his, trail a path of kisses down her slender neck as he held her in his arms.

'Have you finished, sir?'

He flinched as the waiter's arm appeared at his side.

Finished? Unless he lost his mind, he had no intention of starting.

'Oh. Um… Yes, thank you. The steak was perfect.'

He met Clair's knowing look across the table, and knew by the heat his cheeks were flushed. She was as astute as her husband; he'd bet she wasn't easily fooled. He had to try.

'Great restaurant. I'll keep it in mind for entertaining.'

Thankfully the wine waiter distracted her as he topped up her glass. Matt noted Lauren declined.

As they left the restaurant Clair caught his arm.

'I like her, Matt. She's very natural, down to earth. Pity she'll be returning to Sydney.'

'It's her home.'

'Adelaide used to be.'

He didn't answer. He hadn't known.

Duncan hailed a cab, telling Matt they'd drop him and Lauren at the office on their way. As they said goodbye Clair tapped Matt's arm through the window.

'We'll see you Saturday night. I do so love dressing up for corporate dos.'

'I'll be wearing my best tuxedo.'

He took Lauren's arm to guide her into the building, and sensed her guard was back up. Which made his burgeoning idea even more incongruous.

Lauren strove to keep her emotions under control in the lift, fought to keep her fingers from fisting. She didn't have proof yet, only assumptions. Saying anything would detract from the positives of the day.

Matt unlocked his office door, moved aside to let her enter then suddenly stiffened and caught her arm.

'You're trembling. Why?'

She looked into concerned blue eyes, and was swamped by the desire to caress the shadows away from underneath, to ease his burden. To say it was all okay.

'It's been an eventful day. I'd better get back to work.'

'Hmm, and I have to check in with Joanne and the others.' He let go, shrugged off his jacket, and hung it on his chair. Halfway back to the door, he swivelled round and gave her an ironic smile.

'I know I haven't been the easiest of people to work with or approach since taking charge. You're a courageous lady, Lauren Taylor, and I will find a way to repay you for stepping in for me.'

His unexpected compliment threw her. Her first opinion of him eroded a little more as new aspects of his enforced position emerged.

Opening up to her on Thursday wouldn't have been easy. He'd been forced by circumstances to take her into a confidence he'd rather have kept private. Something he only shared with those close to the family.

She went to her desk, determined to crack this puzzler and alleviate the pressure he was under. Her life in Sydney was on hold, her friends were there. When she returned everything would revert to normal. Except her vague fantasy was now a handsome, magnificently built real live male whose aroma, and every look, every touch weakened her knees and sent her pulse skyrocketing.

Her professionalism partially blocked him out at the office, and she managed to focus when dealing with hotel staff and other people. During those hours he was like an undercurrent in her head, surging to full force as soon as she was alone. With his muscled torso—clearly defined under his shirt—his trim waist and flat stomach, his image flicked through her mind like pages of a fireman calendar.

She'd succeed and then she'd have to leave him behind.

Matt returned to his office an hour later. Talking plans and strategies hadn't kept his thoughts from straying to Lauren. The way her chin lifted when she became defensive. The way her hair swung across her shoulders when she turned her head. Her soft hazel eyes betraying every emotion.

They'd crossed a threshold today, and he wasn't sure where it might lead. Surely they could become friends and stay platonic? Yeah, tell that to whatever part of his body was revving up his pulse and stimulating his libido. Initiating a closer relationship while she worked for him was fraught with danger.

She leant forward over her desk as if being closer would make something happen, her eyes riveted to the screen. Delightfully intense. She hadn't noticed his arrival, and started when she did, falling back with her hand covering her heart.

'Sorry, I didn't mean to disturb you.'

She'd gone a delicate pink again, a shade fast becoming a favourite of his. Leaning on the door jamb, he wondered how far it spread, immediately banishing the enticing image.

'I've got a call to make then we'll talk.'

Why? Lauren blinked, stretched, and changed her mind about going for a cold drink. She did a few leg raises, wriggled her fingers, and resumed work.

She tried to ignore the steady drone of his husky voice, interspersed with laughter and long pauses. The gentle tone she'd never heard him use before implied it had to be a woman he cared for. Her stomach knotted and her fingers curled. If she'd dared, she'd have closed the communicating door so she wouldn't have to hear.

His call ended, and she sighed with relief, entered a date for checking, and scrolled down peering at the screen. Neck tingles alerted her as he walked in and sat on the edge of her desk.

Letting her hands fall into her lap, she looked up. Her throat dried, and she wished she'd gone for that drink. Her chest tightened under the intensity of his gaze. It was as if he were searching for her innermost secrets.

'Do you have plans for Saturday night?'

'What?' She jolted upright, gripping the armrests for support. Stared, mouth open, too shocked to think.

His sudden wide smile confused her more, sending her body temperature soaring. Heart-stoppingly handsome before, even with the ravages of fatigue, he was elevated to drop-dead gorgeous.

'It's a simple question. Are you free on Saturday night?'

'I may not be here by then.' Breathless and throaty, not sounding like herself at all.

'No.' Sharp. Irascible. 'No.' Gentler, more controlled. 'Even if you find the cause of the anomalies, there'll be tidying up to do.'

'Why are you asking?'

What could he possibly want from her?

His light chuckle skimmed across her skin.

'I'd like you to be my partner at a corporate dinner.'

'Dinner? Why me?' Her common sense brain patterns seemed to have deserted her.

He leaned forward, and what little breath she managed to inhale was pure ocean breeze.

'A thank you for having my back today. Duncan and Clair like you, and we'll be at their table.'

'Surely there's someone else you could take.'

'After seven years away and working up to eighty hours a week? Anyone I knew is long spoken for. My sister only consented to accompany me out of pity.'

His sister. She flopped. She'd been jealous of his sister.

No! Not jealous.

'Well?' His eyes were like laser beams searching for the answer he wanted.

'Won't she be disappointed?'

'Ah, that's where my negotiating skills came in. I've offered to babysit my two nephews, and shout her and her husband dinner at the restaurant of her choice. She'll have a romantic evening for two instead of set menu, speeches and dancing with her brother.'

Dancing. In his arms.

Too close. Too dangerous. You're already in too deep. Say no, thank you.

The phone on his desk rang. He muttered a low hoarse sound, and appeared reluctant to move.

'Will you come with me, Lauren?'

'Yes.'

Wrong. Idiot. Wrong.

He stroked a feather-touch path down her cheek, immobilising her senses, then smiled again, sending them all haywire.

'Thank you. I promise you won't regret accepting. Do you want to take an early leave? You've had an eventful day.'

'I'm fine. I'll keep going, and you need to reply to that call.'

Fine didn't come near to describing how she felt. Adrenaline coursed through her veins, her lungs were having trouble pumping air and her heart was pounding. And she couldn't tell if it was joy or fear driving them.

Matt had avidly watched the ever-changing emotions in her eyes. Confusion, surprise, shock when he mentioned his sister, and then pleasure as she blurted out her answer. It was as if she were afraid her brain would rebel and refuse his request if she dithered any longer.

He'd gripped the desk to prevent his arms reaching for her, the urge to hold her stronger than he'd ever felt. And then what? He had no idea; with her he was in uncharted waters.

He was, however, determined that before he let her go he'd persuade her to reveal her inner torments, and help her overcome them. He knew with an innate certainty the inner woman was as beautiful as her outward appearance.

Lauren arrived early the next morning even though she'd taken extra time on her hair and make-up. She'd fallen asleep thinking of ball gowns—she'd have to buy one, plus matching accessories—romantic music and dancing with a stunning male in tailor-made formal wear.

It had been dark when she'd woken, her mind buzzing with an idea generated by her discussion over the phone with Pete in Sydney. Eagerness to try it had warred with the desire to look extra good for Matt, so she'd skipped breakfast and bought a sandwich on the way.

The disappointment at his absence was countered with optimism that she'd be able to give him the answers he'd requested. Her fingers hesitated over the keyboard. If she was correct, today might be her last day in this room, so close to him. Even when he was elsewhere in the building, she felt his presence, and his unique aroma lingered in the air.

She'd spend the rest of her working life breathing in expectantly and being disenchanted. Not even the same brand would suit because it wouldn't have his essence.

She booted up. She'd promised to do her best for him, and would, even if it meant she lost out.

Matt arrived mid-morning, eager to see her. He was perplexed by her reticence on the phone when he'd called to say he'd been delayed. If she was having second thoughts about Saturday, he'd have to talk her round.

In his hurry to see her he left his jacket in the car. Not caring, he barrelled through his office to her door where her grave expression pulled him up short. Even as the truth hit home his subliminal mind noted she wore extra make-up. Subtle and captivating.

'You've solved it.' It was what he wanted, had hired her for. So why the heaviness in his chest, and the sudden nausea attack?

She nodded and he swung away to fetch his chair, wheeling it over to her desk. His gut told him it wasn't good and he braced for the worst. Her delicate fragrance taunted him with every intake of air.

Her blue screen was blank except for a familiar symbol.

'And this is…?' He already knew—wanted confirmation yet dreaded receiving it.

Lauren hesitated, hating that what she was about to reveal would hurt him, She had no choice, pressed enter, and a box with a request for a password appeared.

'It's deliberate and there are limited people who had access. Joanne said—'

'You've discussed this with her?' His body surged forward. Anger flashed in his eyes, giving them more animation than she'd seen since they met.

'No! We shared a coffee break yesterday, and she said they'd lost good employees. You referred to the staff turnover last Thursday.'

'I did. I apologise.' It was terser than he'd been lately, with no relenting of his indignant stance.

'It wasn't gossip. Joanne admires your father very much. I got the impression his health had worried her for ages. She said how well he and the staff got on, what a great boss he was, and that he'd installed a number of the programs himself.'

'I didn't know. I wasn't here.' He ground one fist into the other palm.

'It has to be my father.'

CHAPTER SIX

His world had imploded at the sight of the icon. This was confirmation of the suspicion that had grown as he'd checked the records, hoping his father's worsening dementia had been responsible for the unaccountable swings. Saying the words out loud enforced the actuality.

He moved closer and typed in the heading on the plaque in his father's home study, his fingers surprisingly steady in contrast to the agitation in his gut. Two screen changes and he had the answers he needed. And a whole new bunch of complications.

Elbow on the desk, hand clenching his jaw and mouth, he gaped at the folder titles, anger building at the subterfuge of the man he'd admired. What the hell had he been planning?

'Would you like me to leave while you examine the files?'

He didn't turn, couldn't face her. Needing air and time to come to terms with the harsh reality in front of him, he pushed away from the desk, shot to his feet and swung away from her.

'No. Close it down.'

He strode out of both offices, his mind churning with distasteful words: fraud, embezzlement, jail. Ignoring the lift, he went to the stairwell and headed down. There was no more doubt, no more hope of technical glitches, or outside scamming.

If he reported what they'd found his father would be investigated. If he didn't…not an option. He'd fight like hell to save the company and his new enterprise with Duncan but the appropriate authorities had to be informed. Whatever the cost to his own personal reputation, everything had to be open and above board.

He wasn't sure how many floors he pounded down and up again. As his head and his options became clearer, he realised he'd left Lauren in the lurch. She'd succeeded in the task he'd given her, and he'd growled and walked out. Had she left? Would she equate him with his father?

His angst eased a little when he found her sitting by the window in her office writing in a small notebook. She raised her head and he gazed into sweet hazel eyes, full of compassion and offered with complete sincerity. A haven from the tempest.

Lauren sat stunned after he'd barked out the order to shut down and stormed out. He hadn't even glanced at her, just bolted.

After closing down and writing out instructions to access the files, she went for a drink of water, pondering her future, which might be closer than she'd expected. She'd done the job, found what the anomalies hid. Not knowing what the folders contained, she assumed they'd need to be audited, and that wasn't her expertise.

Did this change his invitation for Saturday night? Would she be starting her exploration of rural South Australia earlier than anticipated? She was no longer required so why didn't she feel the usual elation of success? The bubble of enthusiasm for the next assignment?

She took a notebook from her bag and tried to makes notes and failed. Her mind was on the distraught man who was trying to come to terms with his father's deceit. This was a major blow for him. He deserved privacy to come to terms with tangible proof of his father's duplicity and the fallout effects to his family.

His entrance was as abrupt as his departure. He paused for a second in the doorway then walked slowly towards her, midnight-blue eyes dark and unsure of his reception. Her skin tingled, and her heart somersaulted. She trembled as she met his gaze, stood and dropped the book and pen onto the chair.

He took her hands and squeezed them, his Adam's apple convulsing, and his mouth opening and shutting without sound. Slowly, gently he caressed up her arms to hold her shoulders, and inched closer. He stroked her cheek, caught a strand of her hair and twined it round his finger. When she placed a hand on his chest, he shuddered.

If Lauren's heart swelled an atom larger, it

would burst from her body. Heat spiralled from deep in her belly, drying her throat, searing her from within. He evoked feelings she'd never have believed herself capable of, made her aware of a physical wanting she'd only read of in books. He coloured her dreams in brilliant shades and sunshine.

His eyes were searching for her soul and she couldn't look away. Mesmerised by their power, she leant forward in a mirror image to his movement. Stilled when he straightened up, a guttural sound coming from deep in his throat. His hands dropped to his sides, leaving her cold where his fingers had been.

'I... This... *Hell.*' Forceful. Passionate. 'I'd planned for a special lunch with you so we could talk.'

He rubbed the back of his neck and his face contorted as he stared at the computer.

'I have to deal with this now and find out what he's done.'

She understood the battle he was fighting—his family's good name was in jeopardy—but it hurt. She felt as if she'd been dismissed. Gathering up her pen and book, she moved to the desk for her bag and took a sheet of paper from the top drawer.

'These are the access instructions.' She put it on the desk top, Had to get out before she broke down and cried.

'Lauren?' The anguish in his voice tore at her

heart. She turned and saw a different battle in his eyes, one that clogged her throat and tripped her heartbeat.

'Thank you. I may not seem grateful at the moment but I do appreciate all you've done.' He gestured at the computer. 'If possible we'll have lunch tomorrow or Friday.'

'I'd like that.' Much, much more than like.

'There can't be much you don't know or haven't guessed so you must know the ramifications could send us under.'

The potency had gone from his voice, giving him an endearing vulnerability, making her care for him even more. With his strong will, it would only be a temporary effect of the devastating blow.

'If there's anything I can do.' She moved forward until she inhaled his cologne. She was so going to miss the fragrance. The walks she always enjoyed along windswept beaches, especially prior to an impending storm, were going to be a mixture of pleasure and pain for ever.

His rueful smile made her long to wrap her arms around him for comfort.

'I'm sure there will be at some stage. There's nothing now so take a few hours off.'

When she left he was talking on his mobile, an open file on her screen in front of him.

The size of the hidden program astounded Matt. There were accumulated folders and files dating back six years, money transferred in, none out. He studied names and figures, made calls to his accountant, lawyer and Alan. No amount of trying could curb the resentment at his father's deception beginning long before the onset of his dementia.

Cheating was unjustified, in any form. Marcus, acquaintances, even friends deemed nothing wrong with bending rules or breaking promises. A few months ago he'd let himself be fooled by a scheming woman, and had been on the verge of pledging his life and honour to her. She'd claimed to love him, a blatant lie.

Now he was more cynical, and had no faith in romantic declarations. He'd make that clear before entering into any relationship. No emotions, no lies, and nobody got hurt.

Which meant no involvement with Lauren. She was a for-ever kind of girl who'd weave romantic dreams around kisses and…hell, again he'd come so close to kissing her today.

It might be for the best that she'd be leaving soon. It wouldn't be until he was sure there was nothing else hidden, and not until he'd treated her to a night she'd always remember.

He clicked the mouse, and rechecked the folder list. He'd need hard-drive copies of everything plus paper copies of the folder list, maybe others. Lauren's help would be invaluable as he dealt with any authorities who'd have an interest in any aspect of the clandestine accounts.

Bracing himself, he accessed another file, and resumed his onerous task.

Lauren rarely shopped for social events. Her new 'uniforms' of trouser suits and blouses were purchased in the January and June sales. Outside work she wore casual clothes, unless on special occasions. What she did have was in Sydney but nothing in her wardrobe came close to being suitable for a corporate dinner.

She fluctuated between longing to go and fearing she'd embarrass him as she wandered from shop to shop, sifting through racks of dresses and tops. Standing in the change rooms of an international brand store, she almost gave up.

Why this alien urge to buy something bold and extravagant? *So* not her, sleek and clinging, showing off every curve and a seemingly long expanse of leg? Like the low-cut sapphire-blue on the wide-eyed image staring at her from the mirror.

'Do you require any assistance?' the salesgirl called through the door.

No. Though, if she were ever to wear anything like this out in public, a huge hike in self-confidence would definitely help.

'I'm fine, thanks.'

She found what she was searching for in a small off-the-mall boutique. A dress that fitted perfectly and boosted her self-esteem, one she hoped would make Matt proud to escort her. Shoes and a matching clutch bag were bought in a nearby shop, and by mentioning Joanne's name she managed to book an appointment for Saturday at her recommended hairdresser.

Stepping towards the kerb to hail a taxi, she remembered he'd spoken of lunch, a special lunch for two. She dropped her arm and headed back into the mall.

The driver who took her and her parcels to the hotel waited and drove her to the office. She'd rather be there helping him than on her own in her impersonal rented room.

Lauren watched the file names speed through as they were copied to the second hard drive, so many more than she'd expected. Surely this would have a huge effect on the company. Had any of it been declared to the tax office?

She'd be long gone before anything official happened. Matt might remember her as part of his father's downfall, not much more.

He'd been making and taking calls since she'd returned to the office, a pleasant background to her thoughts. She was going to miss his gravel tone when she left. Rougher under stress; she doubted it would ever be smooth. Not even in moments of passion. Which she so should not be thinking about. Ever.

He was absent when she'd finished so she made herself a cup of tea. The man who walked in as she deposited the used tea bag in the bin was tall, handsome and had to be related. His resemblance to Matt was striking, and his instant smile in a familiar face reminded her of Matt's when he'd invited her to the corporate dinner.

Hi, is Matt here?'

'Right behind you, mate.'

She watched enviously as the two men hugged and slapped shoulders, indicating a very strong bond.

'I've made a couple of calls, thought I'd come round to talk. It's quieter here than my office. Then I'll shout dinner. Shall we make it for three?'

Whoever he was, he spoke to Matt but looked at her, with unashamed interest in eyes that were a much lighter blue than Matt's.

Matt noticed the direction of his gaze, his brow furrowed and his eyes narrowed. For the first time since they'd been in high school, he was loath to introduce his charming cousin to a girl. They walked over to her.

'Lauren Taylor, our computer expert from Sydney. Lauren, my cousin Alan Dalton.'

Her quick glance at him told him she'd heard the edge to his voice that surprised him as well.

'Hello, Lauren.' Alan held out his hand, and she accepted it.

'He said he'd hired an expert from Sydney, didn't say *she* was young and beautiful.'

Matt tensed, his breath lodged in his throat.

She'd never acknowledged the few times he'd touched her, though he'd sensed her reactions. He'd barely been able to hide heat rushes from contact with her.

She certainly didn't seem to mind Alan holding on longer than protocol required while he continued his smooth talk. Bile surged in his stomach. He knew how persuasive his cousin could be and felt an indefinable impulse to move between them, break them apart.

Thankfully Lauren appeared to be impervious to his charms, deftly stepping away as she freed her hand. In fact she wore a similar guarded expression to the one he'd first encountered on the day she'd walked into his office. So perhaps it was all eligible men she had a problem with...not just him.

'Thank you. I have plans for tonight.'

Matt knew she didn't and her words inexplicably pleased him.

'Maybe the three of us could have lunch another day.' Not if Matt could prevent it. Alan was a persistent devil.

'I'll be leaving soon so probably not. Matt, the hard drives are in your top drawer. Excuse me.' She took her drink and went to her office.

'Wait here, Alan.' Matt followed her to the chairs by the window, and dropped onto the vacant one. Her sombre hazel eyes caught at his heart.

'You've finished the copying?'

'Yes, is there anything else you want me to do?'

A hundred things flashed through his mind, none of which he could voice out loud. All of which he'd be happy to participate in with her, however inappropriate. A complete reversal of his earlier decision.

'I have no idea until I've seen the accountant and solicitor. I do know I don't want you to leave yet.'

She smiled, her eyes lit up and he fervently wished his cousin were back in his own office two city blocks away.

'It's heading for five. Go home, and if you want time off tomorrow to shop for the dinner that's fine.'

'About that…'

His finger covered her mouth, preventing her from changing her promise and creating a zing along his arm.

'Alan's waiting. We'll discuss details tomorrow. The function's black tie so it's long dresses, or pants and glittery tops. The women usually scrub up good too.'

'Idiot.' Her stuttered laughter raised the hairs on his nape, made his fingers itch to reach out and pull her from her chair onto his lap. He liked that his teasing had rekindled the sparkle in her eyes.

Feeling happier, he stood up, inhaled her enchanting perfume and fought the impulse to stroke her hair.

'I'd better get back to Alan and pick his brains.' She looked puzzled.

'He studied both law and commerce at university. They make a useful combination and I need all the good advice I can get.'

Alan was perched on his desk checking his mobile when Matt walked in.

'Too busy to make the coffee, huh?' He set the machine for two cappuccinos as his cousin came over to join him.

'I've never been able to work that machine. Too elaborate for me.' Alan leant on the bench, picked up a teaspoon, and twirled it through his fingers.

'How long will Lauren be in town?'

'As long as I need her, and I'd rather she wasn't distracted.'

'You've got to admit she's cute.'

'She's also quiet and dedicated to her job. Not your type at all, cuz.'

The spoon stilled in Matt's peripheral vision. He looked up to find a wide grin and knowing eyes.

'Getting territorial, are we, Matt?' The smile faded as Alan's gaze intensified. 'You *are*!'

'She's here to work—an employee. I have no idea if she's free. I'm strictly solo for a long time. Take your pick of reasons.'

He heard the curtness in his tone, regretted being terse with the one person he trusted unconditionally. The only person he'd confided in when he broke off his relationship. The one secret between them was his father's infidelity and he hadn't been able to admit to his father failings, or his mother's acceptance of them, to anyone.

'Alan, I'm sorry. You've been my rock throughout this mess. Put it down to fatigue and frustration.' And, he admitted to himself, maybe jealousy.

'No problem. I'd have buckled weeks ago.'

They were seated by the window when Lauren came through and said goodbye. Alan replied in kind.

Matt held her gaze for an instant, wishing they were alone. 'Enjoy the rest of the afternoon. I'll see you tomorrow.'

'Definitely territorial,' Alan stated after she'd gone. 'Don't give me the guff you spouted earlier. I know you, Matt Dalton. What's the problem?'

'Trust.'

'Hers or yours? I thought you were over the woman in London.'

'There was really nothing to get over. I was angry as hell that she'd cheated on me but my pride took more damage than my heart. So how do you tell if it won't happen again?'

'I reckon Lauren's worth taking a chance on.'

Matt silently agreed.

Thursday morning was muggy with depressing grey clouds and intermittent showers. It was a perfect day for Lauren's mood as she kept close to the city buildings, avoiding raindrops and dodging umbrellas. Which she'd always hated, even the one she'd received on her last birthday. Transparent and shaped like a dome, it made her feel like one of those stuffed birds you saw in old houses and museums.

She'd been rehearsing how to approach Matt since she'd woken, hadn't found an easy way or the appropriate words. Every hasty decision she'd ever made had brought remorse. Though doubtful, proximity might lead to him remembering their meeting on the balcony. Their lives were different. They were different.

She shook out her light raincoat in the building's entrance and folded it over her arm. Sensible, coherent excuses ran through her head as she entered his office, and scrambled in her brain with one look at his striking features, his toned chest muscles moulded to his light blue shirt, and one long leg crossed over at the ankle as he leant against the bench.

'I've changed my mind.' She blurted it out without a greeting, not allowing him to charm her with his gravelly voice or expressive eyes. Not giving him the chance to captivate her with his smile.

CHAPTER SEVEN

HE TURNED HIS head towards her and his body stiffened. His jaw tightened, eyebrows arched and eyes widened, darkened. His lips curled as he did a slow, oh-so-slow scan from her flustered face to her feet. When he finally looked her in the eyes he wore a wide grin and his raspy voice dropped an octave.

'Is this for my benefit?'

'What? Oh.' So focused on her speech, which she'd stuffed up anyway, she'd forgotten she was wearing the new green dress. At the time of purchase she'd hoped the scooped neckline, fitted waist then flared skirt to just above her knees would impress him. Seemed as if she'd succeeded big time.

'You look too exquisite to be spoiling for a fight, Lauren Taylor. I like the dress. Colour suits you.'

'I thought it...you're trying to confuse me.'

He didn't need to try. A look, a smile, a touch and her brain addled.

'I truly don't think I should be your partner at the dinner.'

The mug in his hand clanked as it hit the bench. In two strides he stood in front of her, a determined gleam in his eye. Close. As close as he'd been on the balcony. If he leant forward...

Blushing at her thoughts, she stepped back, out of range. Maybe not. He had long arms. The long, muscular arms she'd last night dreamt of encircling her as they danced to a Viennese waltz.

His lips firmed as her cheeks warmed.

'Okay. We are going to talk this out now and then forget it.'

With surprising tenderness he took her arm and guided her to the chairs, settling her into one then placing her bag and raincoat on the floor. He sat opposite and didn't say a word until she looked up at him.

'I confirmed you'll be my date when I called in to see my sister last night.'

There was an implacable edge in his tone. His eyes, now alert and locked with hers, were corporate mode. She tamped down her longing to surrender and mustered logical arguments.

'You can phone her. I should never have agreed. I'll get tongue-tied and embarrass you.'

'No, I won't. You're beautiful, intelligent, and the Fords want you there. In fact it was Clair who subtly put the idea into my head.'

He thought she was beautiful? Clair had really liked her? Her heartbeat kicked up.

'It's a woman's privilege to renege, of course, but then you'll be the one who has to break the news to my sister and nephews.'

She lifted her chin and glared at him. He was teasing. The gleam in his eyes was back, more compelling than before, and his lips seemed tantalisingly fuller. It was a complete change from her interview meeting. Did he really believe she'd relent on that flimsy statement?

'Why? You can stay with them another night so their parents can go out.'

'No problem there. The camping trip they decided to have seeing they now had no commitments for the weekend might be. The boys were writing a packing list when I left and I'm not going to be the one to disappoint them.'

'Oh.' Her bubble burst. She broke eye contact, fighting not to hug her stomach to quell its churning as she squeezed her legs together to hide their trembling. She gulped when he leaned towards her, fingers linked between his knees.

'You meet and deal with new people every day, Lauren. Your boss receives glowing reports about your interaction with others. How is this different?'

Because it's not work, not technical. Not transient. She realised she'd linked *her* fingers and was grinding her palms against each other. Stopping the action, she drew in a deep breath.

'Those are usually people who want my help. I fix the glitches and leave. And, yes, there are a few regular clients, and our rapport has built up over a number of visits. Not the same and mostly workers on my level.'

Matt held back the chuckle that threatened to

erupt. She sounded so earnest, so desperate to have him believe she'd be a hindrance. So scared of putting herself in an unfamiliar environment.

'Lauren, it's just a roomful of couples wanting to have a good night out and raise money for charity. There'll be set tables for dinner, then people tend to mix once the dancing starts.'

'That's another thing, the dancing. I'm not sure I can in company like that.'

'Ah. Which worries you, traditional or modern? In the first I promise you won't be pressured to join in. And my experience with modern is there are no rules, and the men with the least coordination seem to have the most fun. Especially after a few good wines.'

Her brow cleared, her stiff posture loosened. He was making headway. She knew about his father's condition and financial deception. If either leaked out saving the company could become almost impossible. And he needed her to understand the evening wouldn't be a prelude to a personal relationship.

'You're smart. You must know Dalton Corporation is in trouble. As things stand, your findings could tip us either way. I've been upfront with Duncan Ford and promised he'll be kept informed of all proceedings. Thankfully he has faith in me.'

He reached out and unclasped her hands, covering them with his.

'Please, Lauren. If it will make it easier to accept, treat the evening as an extension of your assignment.'

The gold specks in her darkening eyes were becoming more pronounced. They brightened and softened with her unconcealed changing emotions. He willed her to agree, his own responses heightened by the softness of her skin under his fingers, and the gentle blush on her cheeks. His pulse quickened, and every muscle felt taut as he willed her to agree.

She raised her chin, and her lips curled into a sweet smile.

'You'll come.' If she still wavered, he'd go down on his knees. And pray no one came in while he was there.

'Only so your sister can have her romantic evening.'

If punching the air wouldn't have seemed patronising he'd have done it. He didn't care about her motive, which he suspected she'd grasped at rather than admit she wanted to come.

'Thank you, Lauren. I promise to give you a night you'll never forget.'

She pulled her hands free and leaned away from him as if needing space and distance.

'So what would you like me to do today?'

'I know it's not your field but Joanne says the day-to-day data is behind. I've got meetings this morning and later this afternoon, which should give me some idea of what repercussions I might be facing. Midday's free so I've booked our table for one o'clock'

Shame flooded Lauren. He was fighting for the future of the company and its employees and she'd dumped her insecurities on him. He'd even allowed time to take her for lunch.

'I'm sorry, Matt. I've been selfish, worrying about myself when you've got much bigger problems.'

He stood and held out his hand, his eyes sending a message that weakened every resolve she'd made, and every muscle in her body. Her legs threatened to buckle as she accepted his assistance to stand.

'I'll forgive you almost anything as long as you keep saying my name, Lauren.'

That would be breaking down another barrier between them, and she wasn't sure how many were left. She smiled and stepped away.

'I'd better go and find Joanne.' Her head had demanded poise and self-control. Her voice had proved breathless and aroused.

Wind had blown the dark rain clouds away, bringing in their place white fluffy banks that drifted slowly across the now bright blue sky. The sun had dispelled the morning chill and raincoats could be left behind. The taxi dropped them off at the gates to the botanical gardens and they walked to the restaurant inside.

There were so many shades of green, so many

different plants and flowers, all fresh and glistening from the showers. Ducks waddled over the lawns and birds swooped from tree to tree, their different calls mingling in the air. For Lauren it had become a magical spring day. Made doubly so by the sight of the shimmering white pavilion at the edge of a pond.

'This is where we are eating?' She drew them to a stop to drink in the image, and fumbled in her bag for her mobile to take a photo, though she knew she'd never forget.

'Here, let me.' Matt took it from her. 'Turn around.'

She faced him, the building behind her, the breeze teasing her hair and her heart twisting while she smiled on his command. Twice for her camera then, to her surprise, twice more for his.

The interior was as pristine. White linen covered the tables and chairs, even extended to the serviettes. Silver cutlery, crystal glasses and a delicate floral centrepiece completed an impressive décor.

They were seated by one of the open arches overlooking the waterfall and pond featuring a reed-covered island and a family of colourful ducks. Matt declined wine, opting to share the water she'd asked for. As the waiter left with their orders she gazed round full circle in awe.

'It's so incredible. I can't believe I never came here in all the years I lived in Adelaide. I have a vague recollection of the zoo so that must have been when I was young.'

'You never came to the city on weekends or in the holidays with friends?' As if that made her unique but not in a good way. 'How old were you when you moved?'

'No and thirteen. My family life revolved around my brothers' sporting events. And before you judge, it wasn't so bad.'

Why was she defending what she'd always decried? Unless she was beginning to understand her own personality's part in it all? She sipped water from the delicate glass and smiled. If she had visited the gardens, it would have been in a plastic bottle on the benches outside.

Matt stretched across the table, stroking her hand with his long fingers.

'Believe me, Lauren, I never make judgements on anyone's family. The reason you're here is proof you can never tell what happens behind closed doors.'

Nausea gripped his stomach as he recalled the moment she'd shown him evidence of his father's duplicity. The secret deals and bank accounts, even the location of a large amount of cash. Preparation for what, a new life with another woman? A suspicion he'd keep to himself as long as he lived.

He gazed into hazel eyes, and found warmth and understanding. Something tight around his heart shifted and softened unexpectedly.

'How do you explain nearly five years of lies and deceit, Lauren? What the hell was he planning?'

'Will he even remember?'

'I have no idea how much is real or how much he's been faking, and I'm praying I can keep the truth from my mother. She's defended his behaviour all my life, and I can't bear to disillusion her.'

He found the simple act of caressing her small, delicate hand comforting. The kitchen could take all the time they wanted; he was in no hurry.

'Does she have to know anything?'

'If there are legal proceedings against him or I fail to revive the business, yes. In either case I won't be able to protect her from the consequences. I've accepted my father is guilty and I'll handle whatever happens as it occurs.'

He noticed the waiter approaching with their meals, grudgingly removing his hand.

'No more work talk. This was intended as a get-to-know-you meal before the dinner.'

Get to know you? Lauren already responded to him in ways she hadn't believed were real, much less that she'd be capable of. He could turn her inside out without any visible effort. He was going to haunt her for ever.

She picked up her knife and fork, and made the mistake of looking into his contemplative midnight-blue eyes. It was as if he were seeking a path out of the quandary he'd been coerced into handling, and she might be his beacon.

He ran his finger over his mouth—oh, heck, the mouth that had covered hers so gently, so masterfully. So long ago.

'So, do you follow the footy at all?'

About to begin eating, she almost bit her tongue. Had he remembered?

'Only as a talking point with clients. Sport's never interested me.'

'What does?' He bit into his bread roll, showing neat white teeth.

'Why the sudden interest?' She heard the words, hadn't meant to say them out loud.

'Indulge me. Saturday night I'll be your escort. It would help if we knew something about each other.'

But we are strangers and I have to keep it that way so I can relegate you to 'memories never to be intentionally accessed'. Ever.

He started on his meal, chewing slowly, and studying her as if committing her to *his memory*. Agreeing to go to this dinner was so one of her worst decisions ever. Though it could turn out to be one of the best.

'Does it work both ways?' Again she voiced her thoughts. She didn't wanted to know, hoped he'd refuse.

'I'm an avid Adelaide Crows supporter, and watched every match on the Internet while I was overseas. I played competitive squash—now I fit in games or workouts with Alan whenever I can, and run. My movie taste is for high adventure, fast action. And there's not much I won't eat.'

Wow, more detail to flesh out her fantasies and spice up her dreams of an unsuitable, never ever for her, completely unattainable man. She instinctively squirmed in her seat and pushed into the back.

'Your turn.' He wasn't going to let her off.

'I rarely watch sport, enjoy any well-made science fiction, and Australian historical movies or series and walk whenever possible. I use a gym on a casual basis. I enjoy spicy food, not too hot, and eat limited takeaway when I'm home.

'And you like your job?'

'I love the challenge of a mystery and the adrenaline rush when I succeed. Unfortunately most jobs are mundane, the result of human error and complications when they try to undo without really knowing what they did.'

She heard her own dissatisfaction. Maybe it was time for a change.

'Is there anything else you'd like to do?'

'I'm not sure. It's a new concept.' She frowned at him then smiled. 'Talking to you might not be good for my career. Where did you live in London? I heard houses and units are super expensive.'

'Correct. I got lucky. I own a one-bedroom suburban flat within walking distance of the Tube. Actually, the bank has a major share, but my name is on the deed. And I could buy a new three-bedroom house in Adelaide for less. It's rented out to a colleague while I'm away, which looks like it's going to be much longer than I anticipated.'

He pushed his empty plate aside.

'New topic: favourite ways to relax.'

Matt didn't mention Saturday night arrangements during their meal or on the way back, and kept the taxi waiting while he came in to pick up the folder he needed for his meeting with the solicitor.

He turned to go, made a move towards her and the air stilled between them. The flash in his eyes triggered a surge in her pulse. She waited, holding her breath. His eyes narrowed, his lips parted then his Adam's apple bounced as he struggled for words. The sound he made was guttural, masculine. She felt its effect skittle down her spine.

'Don't go until I get back, okay?'

She could only nod as his finger brushed her lips and he walked out through the door.

Joanne hadn't been kidding about the backlog but by normal finishing time Lauren had made good progress. She tidied up, then went to the nearby shop and bought a magazine and a packet of chocolate biscuits.

She was curled in a chair by his window, filling in a crossword when he appeared and dropped the folder on his desk.

'Stay right there. Another drink?' He indicated the mug by her side.

'No, thank you.' She closed the book and watched him. She'd expected dejection with the prospect of prosecution for Dalton Corporation, his father or both hanging over him. Couldn't see it in his face or movement.

He sat and stretched out his long legs, taking a deep swallow before putting his mug down.

'That tastes good. Thanks for waiting for me.'

His attitude puzzled her. Blasé as opposed to taut as a wound spring as he'd been most of the time she'd been here. As if he read her mind, he arched his back, linked his hands behind his head and smiled.

Where had the dour, weary-eyed man from ten days ago gone? Only the dark shadows under his eyes and the deep lines around his mouth and eyes proved the strain he'd endured.

'Not the same guy you first met, huh? Your finding that screen has taken away the uncertainty, the unknown factor hanging over every decision I made. Now I have true facts and figures to deal with. We'll be audited and investigated but if we're honest we'll survive.'

'So your meetings went well.'

'I've told the truth, and produced all the records and Dad's medical assessment. Now I can concentrate on the new project while the experts work it all out. My priorities are to keep the company going, even if I change its direction, and to protect my mother from any fallout from Dad's actions.'

He drained his coffee, and stood, pulling her to her feet. Close but not quite into his arms.

'You've already exceeded expectations and completed your original assignment. Now I'm asking you to stay here a little longer in case I need you. Please, Lauren?'

How could she refuse when his fingers clasped hers, his voice dropped low with emotion and the pleading in his eyes wrenched at her heart.

The urge to step closer, reach out and trace his strong jaw line, to feel the slight rasp of his almost undetectable stubble, consumed her. Her pulse fluttered, her legs trembled, and swallowing had no effect on her dry throat.

'As long as you think I can be useful.'

'Thank you.'

A buzzer sounded from the reception area, newly installed for visitors. 'Anyone here?'

'That's for me.' He led her to the door and called out, 'Be right with you,' before giving her a quirky smile.

'No peace, as they say. You go home and I'll see you in the morning.'

He didn't. He called as she walked to work telling her he probably wouldn't be in the office at all. How could such a short sentence turn her day cloudy?

'I wanted to talk to you about tomorrow night. Pre-dinner drinks start at six-thirty so I'll pick you up at your hotel around then. It's only a short drive.'

That meant thirty-four hours until she saw him again. She hid her disappointment with a cheerful voice.

'I'll be ready. Call me when you're nearly there and I'll come down to the lobby.'

'I'm looking forward to it.'

In a crazy way with mixed feelings, so was she.

'I'll see you then, Mr Dalton.'

'The name's Matt, remember?'

Matt. Imprinted on her brain, hero of her dreams. Of course, she'd never forget.

CHAPTER EIGHT

MATT WASN'T A teenager on his first date so why did his heart race, his chest feel tight? Why were his palms sweating? Escorting a colleague to a corporate dinner hardly qualified as a date anyway.

Quit fooling yourself, Matt Dalton. She's not a colleague. She's a beautiful woman you are attracted to. And it bugs you that she's so wary of men like you.

He'd called her as the taxi was pulling into the hotel driveway, wanting to be there when she walked out of the lift. The look on her face as she'd agreed to stay on Thursday was imprinted in his brain.

It had been a mixture of fear and hopeful expectancy. If it wasn't complete delight when he brought her home tonight, he'd deem himself a failure. His aims were to see her smile, hear her laugh. And to develop his bond with the Fords.

Cold and objective maybe, but he'd learned that love and happy-ever-afters were more advertising hype than reality. Tonight he'd forget business, relax and enjoy himself. Lauren would go home with happy memories rather than those of nights spent alone in a hotel room.

The lift came down twice while he paced the foyer. She'd said five minutes, four had passed so...

His jaw dropped, his heart pounded. He looked into big anxious hazel eyes and the resolution to keep the relationship casual and platonic shot into Netherland.

She was exquisite, captivating. Every red-blooded man's dream. From her gleaming newly styled, honey-brown hair framing her lovely face, to her red-painted toes peeping out of strappy gold shoes. Her sunshine-yellow dress, which fell loosely to her ankles from under her enticing breasts, shimmered as she walked towards him. A double gold chain around her neck enhanced her smooth peach skin. And she had to be wearing higher heels because she barely had to tilt her head to meet his gobsmacked gaze.

He took both hands in his and held them out, felt *her* speeding pulse under his thumb, and had to clear his choked throat before he could speak.

'Stunning. Lauren Taylor, you are enchanting.'

Her eyes misted. Her glossed lips—oh, he so wanted to kiss them right now—parted.

'I am?' She was genuinely surprised by his compliment. Didn't her room have mirrors?

The lift beside them pinged and opened. As soon as the occupants left, he ushered her in, facing her towards the mirrored wall, and standing behind her.

'Look at yourself, Lauren. You are gorgeous. I'll be the envy of every male in the room.'

His first aim was achieved as she smiled at their reflections. A soft glow appeared in her eyes and grew until they sparkled, and all apprehension disappeared. His arms ached to wrap around her, and if they didn't leave this instant he most definitely would claim a kiss.

After they'd buckled in their driver handed him the corsage he'd left on the front seat.

'I chose this one without knowing what colours you'd be wearing. It seemed…well, you.'

'It's beautiful, perfect.'

He echoed her words in his head, not referring to the flower.

When she reached out to touch the delicately shaded orchid with its deep purple centre, he caught her hand and slipped it onto her wrist. Resisting the whim to press his lips to her pulse, he compensated by linking their fingers and keeping hold. He gave her the same advice he'd given himself.

'Relax and enjoy the evening. It's one of the biggest events of the year, all profits benefitting children's charities.'

He felt her fingers twitch against his, saw the colour in her cheeks fade. But her eyes were clear and steady when they met his.

'Big crowds are less daunting than smaller ones. They're easier to hide in.'

A puzzling remark that intrigued him. Why wouldn't she want to be seen?

'No hiding tonight. Not that you could looking the way you do. Duncan arranged our tickets, and the other two couples at our table are friends of theirs so you'll be in good company. I'll stay as close as I can and make sure you're never alone.

Which was going to be a pleasant task, not difficult at all.

Matt being close might well be her biggest problem, Lauren thought, floating on air from his compliments. He wore formal wear with an innate ease. Had he been so elegant when he'd kissed her years ago? She could only remember those devastating startled blue eyes.

As the taxi joined the line-up waiting to discharge their passengers, she craned her neck to watch them heading for the entrance. These were the elite, the rich and influential, and the corporate climbers—a mingling horde of people eager to see and be seen by their peers. Unlike her, they'd be at ease with each other or skilled at hiding any nerves.

'Lauren?' She turned her head to find Matt regarding her with a pained expression.

'I'll need that hand to eat dinner.'

With a gasp she realised how tightly she was gripping his fingers, and let go.

'I'm so sorry. Does it hurt?' Mortification stung her cheeks.

He gave a low chuckle and wriggled his fingers. 'My friends will say any damage can only improve my guitar playing.'

The car inched forward, stopped and a uniformed man opened Matt's door. She sidled across as he alighted and offered her the hand she'd squeezed. She felt his strength as she allowed him to help her, felt hot tingles race along her veins as he drew her closer for protection in the throng.

The foyer was a kaleidoscope of colours, bold and lurid, pastel and muted, interspersed with the stark black of tuxedos. The overhead lights glistened off the dazzling displays of precious gems adorning necks, wrists, and fingers, hanging from ears and even woven into elaborate hairdos.

Being part of the excitement was worth the initial sick feeling in her stomach, the harsh dryness of her throat. Matt pressed her to his side in his efforts to manoeuvre them to the designated meeting point with the Fords, and the adrenaline rush was intoxicating.

Even he seemed surprised by the number of people who greeted him and held them up. So many inquired if his parents were attending. Others asked when he'd arrived in Adelaide, how long he was staying, and when they could catch up.

They declined drinks until they'd joined their

hosts, Matt selecting a white wine and Lauren a soft drink. Duncan introduced them to a middle-aged couple then, when the men began to discuss today's games, Clair drew the two women aside and grinned at Lauren.

'And at these occasions they talk sport.' She turned to the other woman. 'Lauren's a computer expert and I'm—'

'A danger to any active program,' the woman cut in playfully.

They laughed and Lauren noticed Matt's short nod of approval in her direction. She'd also felt the reluctance with which he'd released her hand. Or was she reading too much into his protective mode?

The doors to the dining area opened and they were asked to locate their seats. As she began to follow Clair, Matt appeared beside her, drawing her close.

'This is incredible,' she whispered, admiring the ornate decorations on the uncountable number of tables.

The dimmed lights gave everything a magical feel, coloured spotlights played across the room, randomly picking out guests for a second or two then moving on. Classical music was supplied by a string quartet on stage, and along the backdrop hung brightly coloured banners bearing the names of sponsors and the charities that would benefit.

Matt guided her to her seat at a table near the

front and sat alongside. Duncan and Clair were on her left. She swung her head, determined to memorise every detail, and shared a menu with Matt as bread rolls and wine were being served.

'Main course is served alternately, chicken or steak. If you'd prefer what I'm given, we can swap. The other courses are set.'

'Thank you. I'm not keen on steak unless it's well done.'

'Good evening everyone.' A deep voice boomed through the sound system urging latecomers to take their seats so the caterers could begin serving entrees. The welcoming thank-you speech was short and amusing, and the quiet music during the meal allowed over-the-table conversation.

Matt and Duncan made sure Lauren was included and she felt at ease enough to join in. Not often and not unless she was sure of the subject but it felt good. Except when Duncan asked if she had siblings. Giving a quick glance to check Matt wasn't listening, she admitted to three brothers, found herself telling him they were all professionals, two footballers and one cricketer. He seemed impressed, wanted more detail. To her their jobs were no different from hers, his, or any other person's.

As the waiters cleared the dinner plates, people began to move around the room, stopping in small groups to talk or wander out into the foyer. Band gear was set up on the stage and the group began to play a slow ballad.

There was a trickle of couples at first then more and more until the floor was crowded. No room for any more, she thought with relief.

'Dance with me, Lauren.' Matt's eyes gleamed, his breath tickled her ear, and his hand on her bare shoulder evoked a quivering in her stomach that had nothing to do with nerves.

'You promised no pressure.'

'True. If you refuse I won't push. But I'll be disappointed, and regret not having even one dance with you.'

Oh, so smooth. No wonder he'd won the Fords over and, according to Joanne, been very successful in England. She'd regret it too; the difference was she'd always remember.

She stood, and accepted the hand he offered. 'Do you always win?'

'The important battles, yes.' The victorious sparkle in midnight-blue eyes proved he believed this counted with those.

He led her onto the dance floor, and slipped his arm around her waist, enclosing her hand in his over his heart. Her legs trembled and her head clamoured for her to cut and run. Her heart leant into him, taking her body along.

Matt had planned his move. The packed floor gave him the excuse to hold her nearer, move slower. Her body aligned with his perfectly, she followed his steps with ease, and her perfume—or her—stirred feelings he'd been denying all week.

Somehow in the last two days the anger he'd carried for weeks had begun to dissipate. Tonight the pain of betrayal had been replaced by an unfamiliar emotion. It took him a few minutes to recognise the alien feeling as contentment, and a little longer to realise that his thumb was caressing her fingers.

The music stopped, and as other couples split to applaud the band they stayed together, his eyes on her face as she looked towards the stage. She was happier and more relaxed than he'd ever seen her. Suddenly however long she'd be here was too short.

'Lauren.'

Bright hazel eyes met his, her lips parted, and only the first few notes of a classic seventies heartbreaker stopped him from kissing her there and then. The couple behind nudged her and he automatically pressed her closer for protection. Her head nestled on his shoulder, his cheek brushed her hair. And he wanted the music to last for ever.

It didn't of course. The singer announced desserts and coffee were being served, and the band was taking a break. He escorted her back to the table, pleased she seemed as reluctant as he was.

'Duncan's gone walkabout,' Clair said, moving along next to Lauren, beckoning her female companion to join them. 'Are you planning to network too, Matt?'

He ought to, it was the sensible thing to do, the

best action for the company. Their desserts arrived, and he grinned and took his seat.

'And miss double chocolate gateau with strawberries and cream. Maybe after.'

'Have Duncan's too, if you like. I'm watching his weight,' Clair offered.

'You want double delight, Lauren?' he teased and was rewarded with a rosy blush.

'I'm not sure I can handle what's in front of me,' she countered without breaking eye contact and his heart leapt into his mouth. Heat flared in the pit of his stomach, and his fingers itched to reach for her and…

'Coffee for anyone?' A waiter held up cups and saucers on the other side of the table.

Yeah, black and strong for me to drown in. And is that a tiny smirk on her face?

If they were alone he'd be kissing it off in an instant.

'I'll take one, thanks.' Duncan loomed up behind Matt and sat down. 'After that, and the dessert I'm going to be scalded for eating all weekend, I want you to meet a trusted friend of mine, Matt. If we decide to proceed with the bigger project an extra investor might be welcome.'

Matt glanced at Lauren.

'You go. I'll be fine.'

She was. Too much so. Catching up with business acquaintances and meeting new contacts should have been a pleasure but his mind was on

Lauren, and how long he'd been away. He'd left her talking to Clair and her friend. When he returned she was in deep conversation with a blond-headed man who, in his opinion, was leaning too close.

His gut hardened, his jaw clenched and he strode over to where the two of them sat alone.

'Sorry I've been so long, Lauren.' Not much regret in his tone.

They turned, and the man rose to his feet, extending his hand.

'Matt Dalton, isn't it? I'm sure I played high-school footy against you a few times. I'm John Collins, a friend of Lauren's brother. Haven't seen her for five or six years so this was a pleasant surprise.'

Matt's irritation abated and he accepted the greeting.

'Your face is familiar though I can't remember the name. Too many over the years.'

'Yeah, I know.' John glanced at his watch. 'I'd better go find my wife and say our goodbyes. My mother-in-law's babysitting. Great catching up with you both.'

'Where is everyone?' Matt asked as soon as he'd gone, shaking off his discomfort. An old friend of the brother's. Married and bending close, as *he* was now, because of the constant hum of voices combined with the now louder and upbeat music.

'Out there having fun.' Lauren laughed and pointed at the dance floor.

It was hard to tell who was partnering who as

arms were waving, bodies writhing and legs kicking, stomping and twisting. Clair was easily spotted in her bright red dress, grinning and waving as she recognised friends. Duncan, now coatless, followed no rhythm but his enjoyment was clear.

'Let's join them.'

She demurred.

'Look at them, Lauren. No rules. No cares.' He seized her wrists, lifting her to her feet. 'Come on.'

She'd shrunk. He looked down at her stockinged feet. Felt the grin spread across his face.

She grinned back. 'My new shoes started to pinch. Besides, I can hardly dance like that in those heels.'

'Not without spiking someone, probably me. Hang on while I ditch my coat.'

This was the best and the worst idea he'd had all night. The way Lauren's body synchronised with the rhythm created havoc in his. Her dress outlined shimmering hips as she swayed. Her lustrous hair brushed her shoulders as she swung her head and her skin glowed under the spotlights. Even watching her delicate energetic feet with their red tips gave him a warm glow.

Completely in the moment she'd let go of whatever cares she had, given herself to the magic of the music, and was in a world of her own. A world he wanted to be part of for as long as possible. He tasted bile in his mouth at the thought of her leaving, swallowed it down. Emotion-inspired happy-ever-afters were a myth.

'Last dance, ladies and gentlemen. Slow or fast?'

Couples were already coming together, calling out 'slow' and drowning the requests for fast. A few left the floor. Lauren's eyes shone as he stepped closer. She didn't resist at his pressing her head to his shoulder. She was smaller without her heels, making him feel more macho, more protective. He caressed her back, drawing her tightly against him, and swor0e00 he heard a contented sigh.

Lauren sighed again as the taxi eased into traffic. This was an enchanted evening. A night to cherish always, for so many reasons. The man responsible for those unforgettable memories shifted across the seat, put his arm around her, and nestled her into his side.

'Glad you came, Lauren?'

His voice was low, gruff, his breath tickled her ear. She turned, put her hand on his chest, and wished she could snuggle into him and fall asleep. Any dreams she had tonight would surely be pleasurable.

'Mmm, it was wonderful. I didn't want it to end.'

'It hasn't yet.'

Her fingers curled, her heart chilled and she stopped breathing. He didn't think, wouldn't expect... No. That wasn't the man she...could she possibly learn the true man within less than two weeks, four days of which were spent apart?

'We have the drive home and I'll ask the cab to wait while I escort you to your room.'

'There's no need.' Her words came out in a rush of air.

'My pleasure. Would you like to hear the compliments Duncan paid you?'

'He and Clair are nice, so easy to talk to though she made a few enigmatic remarks during the evening, and asked twice how long I'd be here. Said she'd like to meet for lunch before I go. Oh.'

She gasped as he suddenly squeezed her as if annoyed at her remark.

'Don't think about leaving yet. Don't think about anything but tonight. Did I mention you were the most beautiful woman in the room?'

She smiled up at him. He was smooth and charming, handsome as hell and his midnight-blue eyes glowed with an intensity she'd never seen. Ever. From anyone.

'Once or a dozen times. Thank you for everything.'

He tapped the folder under her clutch bag on the seat. 'And you have the photos.'

'They're mine?'

'All yours.'

So he didn't want any reminders. She'd behaved as he'd asked, been a helpful social partner, and he was simply grateful. But in the end she was just the skilled technician hired to fix his system. A chill settled over her. The gloss faded. The evening was tainted.

A few moments ago she'd been elated, not wanting the evening to end. With two simple words, he'd burst her blissful bubble. She felt tired, numb... She wished she were alone, yet contrarily didn't want to leave the warm haven of his arms.

CHAPTER NINE

He put distance between them in the lift as if sensing her withdrawal. She kept her eyes downcast, and hung onto the photos like a lifeline. They and the exotic orchid on her wrist were mementoes she'd treasure for ever.

She should be grateful. She would be, when common sense rid her of the dull ache. Not now. Maybe once they'd shared polite platitudes, and she was alone.

Her key card. She'd better have it out ready and limit any awkward time. The doors opened and he guided her towards her room, turned her to face him, gripping her elbows, his features composed, his eyes dark as ebony.

They held her captive, mesmerised her. Seconds. Minutes. She was drifting, vaguely aware of him freeing her arms.

'Sleep peacefully, Lauren.' Rough as if forced over jagged stones.

Then, like déjà vu, his lips were on hers, moving smoothly yet more masterful, more mature. Like ten years ago their only physical contact. And like ten years ago she instinctively responded, wanting his kiss to last for ever.

Breaking away, eyes now narrowed and puzzled,

he stepped back, and gave a slow short shake of his head.

'Goodnight, Lauren.' He sounded bewildered before walking away.

Had he remembered? Realised who she was? Her hand shook as she blindly tried to swipe her card without taking her eyes off his rigid departing back. She froze as he turned, strode back and yanked her into his arms, taking her mouth with a fierce male grunt. Causing her to drop everything and cling to him.

This wasn't the exploratory tenderness of the teenage boy, or the polite goodnight of a moment ago. This was raw, masculine need, a hunger that swept her up and demolished any inhibitions. He caressed her back in wide strokes, urging her closer, searing her skin wherever they touched.

A yearning to arch into his warmth overwhelmed her. She couldn't breathe, didn't care. Her legs shook, her body quivered, fire flared in her core. And her lips parted willingly as he deepened the kiss.

She tasted wine and rich coffee, a hint of chocolate and—

His head flung back, his chest heaved. His stunned eyes raked her face, and his lips parted without sound. He backed away, arms wide. He hit the wall opposite and swallowed, dark eyes roaming her face as if he'd never seen it before.

With his gaze locked with hers, he came slowly

YOUR PARTICIPATION IS REQUESTED!

Dear Reader,

Since you are a lover of our books – we would like to get to know you!

Inside you will find a short Reader's Survey. Sharing your answers with us will help our editorial staff understand who you are and what activities you enjoy.

To thank you for your participation, we would like to send you 2 books and 2 gifts – **ABSOLUTELY FREE!**

Enjoy your gifts with our appreciation,

Pam Powers

**SEE INSIDE
FOR READER'S
SURVEY**

For Your Reading Pleasure...

YOUR READER'S SURVEY
"THANK YOU" FREE GIFTS INCLUDE:
- ▶ 2 FREE books
- ▶ 2 lovely surprise gifts

PLEASE FILL IN THE CIRCLES COMPLETELY TO RESPOND

1) What type of fiction books do you enjoy reading? (Check all that apply)
- ○ Suspense/Thrillers   ○ Action/Adventure   ○ Modern-day Romances
- ○ Historical Romance   ○ Humor   ○ Paranormal Romance

2) What attracted you most to the last fiction book you purchased on impulse?
- ○ The Title   ○ The Cover   ○ The Author   ○ The Story

3) What is usually the greatest influencer when you <u>plan</u> to buy a book?
- ○ Advertising   ○ Referral   ○ Book Review

4) How often do you access the internet?
- ○ Daily   ○ Weekly   ○ Monthly   ○ Rarely or never

5) How many NEW paperback fiction novels have you purchased in the past 3 months?
- ○ 0 - 2   ○ 3 - 6   ○ 7 or more

YES! I have completed the Reader's Survey. Please send me the 2 FREE books and 2 FREE gifts (gifts are worth about $10 retail) for which I qualify. I understand that I am under no obligation to purchase any books, as explained on the back of this card.

119/319 HDL GLNV

FIRST NAME	LAST NAME

ADDRESS

APT.#	CITY

STATE/PROV.	ZIP/POSTAL CODE

forward and lightly traced shaking fingers down her cheek, settling under her chin.

'Wow.' Incredulous. Deep and husky. He seemed to struggle for breath. 'I…I'll see you Monday.'

By the time she'd blinked he'd gone, heading for the stairs.

Lauren fought for composure, unable to move. What had she done to provoke such a reaction? Where had *her* response come from?

The lift's ping brought her back to the present. She scooped up her belongings and a moment later was secure behind her closed door. Dumping the stuff on the desk, she flung herself onto the bed, reliving every second since they'd exited the lift.

She studied the photo of the two of them, searching for something to explain his behaviour and sudden flight. There was no clue in his open expression or his smile. Nothing to indicate he had anything but enjoying the function on his mind.

So it had to be her. What deficiency did she have in her personality that discouraged more familiar contact? Did she give out negative vibes? She had close friends, some from back at school and uni in Melbourne.

Their common interests had been the original base but their friendships now went much deeper. She knew she could always depend on their support in any situation. It was her family who seemed to find excuses not to be with her. Or was it she who put up barriers, subliminally deterring closer intimacy for fear of being rejected?

She set the photo against the lamp on the bedside table, placed her corsage in front of it, and prepared for bed. They were clearly visible in the light from the street lamps. She fell asleep with her fingers on her lips.

Matt fisted one hand into the palm of the other as the taxi drove him home. He could smell her perfume on his shoulder, see her shocked expression when he'd pulled away and left. He still savoured the taste of her on his lips.

He'd meant that first kiss to be gentle, an affectionate ending to a memorable night. Her initial response hadn't surprised him. Its effect on him had been astonishing. His libido had gone into overdrive and that damn niggle had drummed in his head. Breaking free had been instinctive.

But he hadn't been able to walk away. The invitation he'd seen in her hazel eyes had driven him back and he'd let his pent-up desire run free. He'd moulded her body to his, caressing her back, and exploring the curves he'd delighted in all evening. He'd invaded her mouth, savouring her sweetness, craving more.

Her soft moan had slammed him back to reality. To the shame of his actions. He'd never lost control before. Getting the hell out of there had seemed the only option; now it branded him a coward.

Going back to apologise while he still ached for more intimate contact would exacerbate the pain he'd caused. Phoning would be even more cowardly. He hadn't felt so much like a louse since...

Since the night he kissed a girl hiding in the dark on a balcony. The niggling cleared like a light-bulb moment in his head. An irresistible allure. A barely heard sigh. Soft lips under his.

The kiss he'd never forgotten, had relived so often in his dreams, and that had been so entrenched in his memory that his body had known her the instant their lips had met tonight. He'd never had a face to picture, only a curled mass of dark hair, and a recollection of a slender body in a blue dress. And throughout the ten years since, no lips had ever felt as soft or tasted as sweet.

He'd searched the ballroom for her, and spent the rest of the evening repeatedly scanning the crowd without success. Deep inside he'd never given up hope of finding her.

Now he understood the guarded look and apprehension the day he'd interviewed her. She'd recognised him, must have remembered their meeting as well.

Tomorrow he'd begin to make amends for tonight's ending. Monday morning was going to be very interesting.

* * *

Matt's jacket hanging on the back of his chair was the only indication he was in the building. Lauren wasn't sure if she was upset or relieved.

Tucked into her purse was the florist's card that had accompanied the arrangement of orchids delivered to her hotel room yesterday morning. Another memento, personally inscribed, *Forgive me, Matt.*

For the kiss or for running?

She'd imagined a number of scenarios for when they met again, none of which eased her apprehension. She couldn't shake the re-emerged doubts. Their lives, their interests, their personalities, all were polarised. If it weren't for the undeniable attraction, they'd have nothing in common. She sighed and gazed out of her window lost in a daydream of music, lights and feeling cherished as they'd danced.

'Why were you hiding?'

She jumped, spun round to find him standing halfway across the room. Her heart stuttered. She covered it with her hand, and fought to steady her erratic breathing. How come he looked so cool and calm? So unruffled?

'I wasn't.' She cursed her wobbly voice. 'I'm just doing my normal preparation.'

Three rapid paces brought him an arm's length from her side, leaning on the glass nonchalantly. The firm set of his jaw belied his calm demeanour, giving her composure a tiny boost. He gestured in the general direction of the river.

'On the balcony, a good cricketer's throw away from where we had lunch with the Fords.'

He knew—had to see the blush heating her neck and face, the embarrassment in her eyes. Her teeth as they bit on her lip, something she hadn't done since she was a child.

As she struggled for breath and an answer, his lips—lips that had filled her waking hours since he'd strode away—curled into an apologetic smile.

'I have no idea why I followed you. I saw a mass of dark curls and a hint of blue dress going through the door alone and wondered why. Couldn't find you at first.'

He inched a little closer.

'You running away shook me. I swear I looked for you to apologise, and I've always regretted frightening you but never the kiss, never the sweet taste of your lips.'

'I hated being there,' she blurted out without thinking. 'Hated the way I was forced to be part of a world I had no interest in. Places like the balcony were sanctuaries. I didn't belong inside with those people.'

Fleetingly stunned by her outburst, he recovered to run his fingers in a light path down her cheek and under her jaw, sending fissions of delight skimming across her skin. If he let go, her legs would give way and she'd end up a trembling mess on the floor.

'And I invaded your peace. Did you know who I was before the interview or recognise me then?'

She felt her skin heat again and dropped her gaze, only to have him tilt her head until she looked him in the eyes. His eyebrows quirked.

'Lauren?'

'There were lights behind you that night. I didn't see your face but as I pushed away your eyes became visible. They're very distinctive.'

His low chuckle zinged through her. Laughter shone in his eyes and they crinkled at the corners.

'My eyes, huh. We'll have to talk more but not *here*.'

He grated the last word and then his tone softened.

'The next few days are going to be gruelling. I'll be juggling appointments regarding Dad's actions with meetings, on and off site, about new projects. They'll all take time away from where I want to be.'

His affectionate expression said he meant her. The gap between them diminished. His movement or hers?

'Come to dinner with me tomorrow night.'

There was an edge to his voice that she didn't understand. Her first inclination was to refuse but then she'd always wonder.

He claimed he'd tried to find her. If she agreed—

and her heart and logic warred about the sensibil-
ity of that—she'd have personal time to learn more
about him, be able to return to Sydney with no
what-ifs. His persuasive voice, his hypnotic gaze,
and his touch on her skin were an irresistible combination.

She meant to nod, swayed forward instead. As
if in answer to her silent plea, he bent his head.
Suddenly jerked away.

'Not here.'

Growled in anger. Why?

His fingertips tracked lightly across her neck,
triggering a goose-bumps rush from cell to cell,
from her scalp to the soles of her feet. Awareness
flared in his eyes, his chest heaved, and suddenly
there was a wide space between them.

'I have to make a couple of calls, and talk to
Joanne before I leave.'

'What am I supposed to do after I've finished
the data entries?'

He spread his arms, fingers splayed.

'Whatever Joanna needs help with. I know it
may be below your expertise but...'

He struggled for words. 'I don't want a stranger
coming in when we transfer those accounts into
the mainstream. I want you.'

The inflection in the last three words was personal, nothing to do with accounts or computers.
Leaving wasn't an option.

'I'll stay.' Data entry. Filing. Basic office work.

Tasks that would allow her mind to wander to midnight-blue eyes and smiles that lit up her day.

'You're an angel. I'll be here for half an hour then out for the morning. My mobile will be off most of the time so leave a message if you want me.'

His hand lifted towards her. Dropped. He walked out, picking up his jacket on the way.

If she wanted him?

Her body hummed with a need more disturbing than anything she'd ever felt. So much stronger than the mild desire she'd felt during her two previous relationships. She now recognised them as more mind melding and merely physical rather than zealous ardour.

There'd be no 'let's be friends' when the passion died for Matt. He'd walk away and she...she'd survive. Somehow.

Matt strode to the boardroom, praying it would be empty. He was pleased he'd been able to persuade Lauren to stay. Having her at his home for dinner was risky, considering the way they both responded to the proximity of the other. But how else were they going to talk without interruptions? How else could he find out why she hadn't trusted him before she knew him?

He'd almost kissed her again this morning. Never, ever going to happen here. He would never follow in his father's footsteps. Would never use that bedroom, no matter how late he worked or how tired he became.

Footsteps sounded in the corridor. He refocused on the project he and the team were working on, the one he was determined would revitalise the company.

Everything hung on a precipice. His father could be facing fraud charges. He and, in his doing, Dalton Corporation had probably committed tax evasion. Duncan Ford might decide to suspend their talks of investing until Matt could prove he and the company were clean.

He should be broken, anxious of the future. Instead, now he knew the truth he found the challenges stimulating. If it all collapsed around him, he'd start again. Staying down wasn't an option.

Lauren collected information needed from Joanne's office and settled at her desk. She tingled from his touch, her stomach had barely settled, and her brain was in the clouds.

Logging in took two attempts at the password. When she went to write the date on her notepad, she'd left her pen in the drawer. Unless she pulled herself together, today would be a shambles.

Get it together, Lauren.

A fingertip tap on each of her work tools, a muscle-loosening back-stretch, followed by her slow-count-to-fifteen habit, and she moved the cursor.

Engaged in more simplistic tasks, she found her mind had a tendency to wander, always to Matt and his effect on her. After an hour, she took a break, ran up and down eight flights of stairs and refocused. Apart from taking messages from occasional phone calls, she was undisturbed.

At midday she joined Joanne and three of the male staff for lunch for the first time, making an effort to contribute to the weekend football match discussion. She didn't comment when one of the men raved about her youngest brother, who'd kicked four goals including one as the siren sounded.

'Mr Dalton seems happy with the progress we've made on this new venture, Joanne. It's completely different from anything we did for his father, quite stimulating. Do you think the changes will be permanent?'

Lauren lowered the mug she'd been raising to her lips. She noticed Joanne's hesitation at the man's question. How much did she know of the true situation?

'I know he's doing all he can to sort everything out and he'll be tied up with meetings most of the week, nothing else.' She rose and went to stack her utensils into the dishwasher. 'Break's over. Do you have enough to do, Lauren?'

'Yes, I'll find you if I need more.'

Every employee she'd met addressed him as Mr Dalton. Although he used their first names, he kept distance between himself and his staff except for her. Because he intended to return to London?

Was there someone special there? Someone prepared to wait for him? Someone he'd taken to Paris?

A no-strings arrangement by two mature people. How did they do that? She couldn't imagine becoming involved with anyone who also dated other women.

Reinforcing that in her head didn't stop her stomach from fluttering at his call sign on her mobile.

'How's it going, Lauren?'

'Fine. Joanne says she can keep me occupied today and part tomorrow, after that I may be on cleaning duty.'

He laughed as she'd hoped he would, deep and raspy, making her ear tingle.

'Anything to keep you here. I won't get to the office until late today, or tomorrow morning. I'll call you when I can.'

'Is it bad?'

'I'm dealing with reticent legal and financial professionals. They hardly commit to black or white coffee but at least it's not all doom and gloom. Hang on.'

She heard his name and him replying, 'Thank you.'

'I'm being summoned back to the world of ifs, maybes, and it all depends. I'll see you tomorrow, Lauren.'

'Tomorrow.'

She sat as still as stone, staring at her mobile. He'd called her Lauren twice; she hadn't said his name at all. He used hers every time he spoke to her. At the function she'd made a deliberate attempt to say 'Matt' in the presence of others. In front of work colleagues it was 'Mr Dalton', to conform with them. Alone with him she omitted to call him anything.

He was smart, quick to notice nuances and actions. He'd have to know she deliberately avoided the intimacy of first names.

CHAPTER TEN

MATT DIDN'T WANT to be sitting in his parents' dining room that night pretending nothing had changed. His head ached from all the legal jargon, the implications of what might or might not happen, and from reading some of the complex forms and documents he'd been given. And the processes had only just started.

It had taken supreme effort to keep focused and not picture Lauren alone in her office or Joanne's. Or ponder on dinner tomorrow. No disruptions, no phone calls with both mobiles on silent. Quiet time for conversation.

It's more than talk you want.

'Matthew?'

'Sorry, Mum. Miles away. It's been a long day.'

'This is all taking a toll on you. I wish I'd acted sooner, but Marcus kept assuring me he was just tired and overworking.'

'It's okay, Mum. I've got good help and everything's coming together.'

Though there's a fair chance it might implode in my face.

'His mood swings are more frequent, and persuasion doesn't work as well as it did. Today he became angry when I suggested he shouldn't go for a walk alone.'

His jaw tightened, and he glared at his father, nonchalantly eating his meal. He softened his features as he asked, 'When's his next appointment with the doctor? I'll make sure I'm available and then we'll have a family meeting.'

'I want to keep him at home as long as possible. Please, Matthew.'

He reached across to cover her hand with his.

'For as long as possible, Mum. We can arrange for day help and, if necessary, I'll move in.'

His gut churned at the thought of living here again, in the house where his naive adulation of his father had been shattered, and his admiration for his mother diminished in a single stroke. Where he'd discovered human weakness could overrule honour, and betrayal could be overlooked if it meant the continuation of a preferred lifestyle.

His honour dictated he had no choice. His heart demanded he call into his sister's on the way home to spend time with a truly happy couple. And to kiss his nephews as they slept.

Crouched behind the desk in Reception, Lauren almost missed Matt's arrival at five past two the following day. Checking the stationery, she sprang upright at the faint hint of sea-spray aroma.

'Matt.' Instinctive. Spontaneous.

As natural as the smile he gave her. He looked

frazzled and energised at the same time, jacket slung over his shoulder and sleeves rolled up to reveal muscular arms covered with fine dark hair. One glance at finger-ruffled hair and blue crinkled eyes, and her senses sprang to attention.

'Hi, how's it going? Come and tell me over coffee. With normal everyday words.'

'Joanne's run out of work to give me.' She straightened the desk phone as she glanced up, and met narrowed eyes and a scowl.

By the time she come round to his side, they'd gone. He patted his satchel as they walked to his office. 'And I'll be occupied for days. How's your legalese?'

'My what?'

'Legal mumbo jumbo. Guaranteed to cause headaches or a craving for alcohol.'

She laughed. 'Sorry, all I know is the few foreign phrases I learnt from friends at uni. Unless it's cyber-speak.'

'Might just as well be for me. So what time are you finishing?'

'Ten minutes and I'm all done.' She swallowed, glad he wasn't looking at her. Thankful he couldn't see her disappointment.

His brow creased again as he held the door open for her, not moving aside, ensuring she brushed against him as she passed. He dumped his satchel on his chair, draped his coat over the back, and scraped his fingers into his hair. When he spoke she swore there was a catch in his voice, growing more pronounced towards the end.

'You're not going home?'

She shook her head. 'I promised I'd stay.'

'You're one of the few people aware of the full situation and I trust you. We'll find something for you to do.'

He trusted her. Her heart soared and dipped, raced for a moment then blipped. She couldn't deny she had continuing issues with where he'd come from, the class he associated with.

'You don't have to. I decided last week to spend my promised fortnight vacation being a tourist in South Australia.'

His face cleared and he caught her hands in his, skittled her breathing with his beaming smile.

'Two weeks, huh? That's good. Can you fit any work I need done between trips?'

'If I'm needed.'

'You are—very much.' His intense appraisal was unnerving, as if commanding she hide nothing from him. His undisguised admiration made her insides glow, yet roused a prickling unease on her nape.

'Is there a special dress code for tonight?'

'Neat casual. Whatever you feel comfortable in.'

Your arms.

Thankfully thought and for once not voiced. She cursed her seesawing responses.

'I'll call when I leave here and pick you up.'
'I'll be ready.'

She was sitting on a bench near the revolving doors two minutes after he phoned. It gave her a clear view of the curved driveway and the road beyond the garden bed. Her fingers tapped on her right thigh and she clasped them with her left hand.

It was just another dinner in a public place, nothing to make her nervous. Unless you counted the confident, charismatic male striding, head high, on the opposite side of the road. At twenty-six, she really ought to be able to control these sudden spikes in her pulse and these inexcusable urges to run to meet him.

She went to the kerb, keeping track of him between passing vehicles. He stopped when he noticed her, his smile easily visible at this distance, and beckoned her to come across. Took her arm as she reached his side.

'Hi, has anyone ever told you that you are remarkably punctual?'

'For a woman?' She tilted her head, and raised her eyebrows. Relished the pleasurable quiver in her stomach as he laughed.

'For a human. The car's not far.'

He didn't speak during the short walk, obviously preoccupied. Lauren was all too aware of his guiding touch on her arm. Warm and protective.

The lights flashed to unlock his car but he didn't open the door. He leant on it instead, placing his hands on her waist. He looked at the grass under their feet and exhaled.

'When I said dinner, I meant takeaway or home delivery to the unit I'm renting. You and me. No phones, no demands from anyone. No distractions. I should have been explicit. If you'd prefer, there's a local hotel with good food and friendly atmosphere.'

His preference matched hers. No noisy chatter or waiters hovering to serve, clear dishes or top up glasses.

'Do I get to choose what we pick up?'

She hadn't realised how tense he was until his shoulders dropped.

'Food, wine and anything else you want.' He moved aside, allowing her to get into the car. 'You amaze me almost every day, Lauren Taylor.'

Lauren was the one surprised as she entered the modern single-storey town house not far from the city. He'd driven into the garage, led her through the door into a laundry and then along a hallway into one of the most sparsely furnished rooms she'd ever seen.

There was a long soft leather lounge, a coffee table and a television on a wooden cupboard. No rugs, no cushions. No books, ornaments or pictures.

She appreciated he was renting, and had been working long hours under extreme pressure, but…

Matt's eyes followed her astonished gaze, and for the first time he saw his home as it was. He'd bought the barest necessities, hadn't been planning on long term or entertaining.

He shrugged and gave a rueful grin.

'Not exactly home beautiful, but I don't spend a lot of time here.'

'Are the other rooms the same?'

Leaving the Thai food and bottle of white wine on the table, he held out his hand.

'Guided tour included with the meal. Any constructive opinions welcome.'

She didn't say a word as he pushed open doors to reveal a desk and office chair in one room, suitcases and boxes in another, the bathroom, and finally the main bedroom.

It contained bedside drawers and a rumpled king-sized bed, which dominated the space but he never slept well in anything smaller. Since moving in he'd crashed every night into deep, unbroken sleep, including a few times in the lounge. Except for the last two nights, and his restlessness was evident from the unmade bed.

His senses were on super alert, tuned for her slightest reaction. He heard the faint intake of breath, saw her shoulders twitch and the convulsive movement in her throat.

Berating himself for his insensitivity, he drew

her away, and pulled the door shut behind them, praying she didn't think he had an ulterior motive bringing her here. He couldn't ignore the picture that had flashed into his head as he'd looked from his bed to Lauren, or its effect on his body.

'I signed the lease in the morning, made the saleswoman's day in the afternoon, and moved in two days later,' he said, hoping to distract her as he took her to the kitchen area.

'No dining setting?'

'Not yet. The only person who visits is Alan, and we eat while we watch TV, usually the footy.'

She winced and he remembered her outburst yesterday morning. She hadn't exaggerated her dislike of sport. Tonight he was determined to find out why.

'We'd better eat before the food goes cold. Plates are in the corner cupboard. I'll bring the glasses and cutlery.'

Clicking on the TV, he scrolled to the relaxing music channel, keeping the volume low. He sat, giving her space, and opened the Riesling, poured a glass and slid it in front of her.

'Thank you. I'm guessing you like leftovers, from the amount of food you bought.'

'It'll taste as good tomorrow.' He lifted his glass in salute. 'To you, Lauren. You have my eternal gratitude for everything you achieved.'

She tapped her glass to his. 'Even with all the angst it's going to cause you?'

'Hard facts can be dealt with. The uncertainty is what fuels suspicion and creates tension. I'll be guided by the professionals and handle any repercussions.'

Lauren savoured the tang of the sweet and sour pork, and the mellow taste of the wine, but found the depth of the settee uncomfortable. It was built for taller people or for curling up on. A few thick cushions would solve the problem.

She put her plate on the table, slid onto the floor, and folded her legs.

'Can we pull this closer so I can lean against the sofa? I don't have your long limbs.'

He complied immediately. 'I'm not rating too well, am I? I'm all set up for myself, didn't expect to have visitors very often if at all.'

Then why that huge bed, looking as if there'd been plenty of action there last night? Did he have similar expectations tonight?

She choked on a piece of pineapple, took a soothing drink of wine, letting it glide down her throat. He'd said only Alan visited and she had no reason to dispute his word.

'Are you all right?'

No, but admitting it might start a conversation she wasn't ready for, probably never would be.

'I'm fine. This is delicious.'

'Hmm.' He relaxed, elbow on the leather arm, his legs stretched out with one ankle over the other. Looking as hassle-free as a newborn baby.

Unlike her. Sitting down here might be easier on her spine but now he was only in her peripheral vision and other senses heightened. She became aware of muted sounds as he shifted or flexed muscle against the leather, and his ocean aroma teased her nostrils, overriding the piquant sauces of their meal. Occasionally his foot twitched.

The companionable silence stretched, the music soothed. She picked up her glass and sipped, letting her mind drift to a gentle touch, a guiding hand. A bewitching dance she'd never forget.

She turned her head, and caught him watching her, his lips curled, his dark eyes gleaming with unconcealed desire. He blinked and it vanished. Or had it been a reflection of her own?

'Full?'

She could only nod, her throat too clogged to form words. He wanted to talk; she'd prefer to delay it any way possible. If he wanted her history, dared she ask for his? Wouldn't it be better to have only memories of *their* time together untainted by his past?

The dishwasher was stacked, the food containers stored in the refrigerator. Lauren curled up in the corner of the settee cradling the remnants of her drink.

'Top up?' Matt waved the bottle in front of her.

Why not? She'd make it last 'til the end of the evening.

He half-filled hers, gave himself more then took

the remainder to the fridge. Settling at the far end, he twisted towards her, one ankle balanced on the other knee. His arm lay along the back of the lounge, forming a perfect angle with his body for someone to snuggle into.

She stifled the sigh that threatened as she remembered the firm warmth of him, and the way her head rested cosily on his shoulder during the slow dances. A quick self-rebuke, a sip of wine and she met his gaze with a bravado her internal fortitude didn't match.

'So you didn't inherit the sporting gene like your brothers?' A coaxing tone, probably developed with his nephews, with an edge that said he wouldn't give up until he'd learned all he wanted to know.

'I was uncoordinated, couldn't catch, throw or jump and had no interest in being coached to improve. Lately I've been wondering if I was the one who withdrew from my family rather than it being them who ignored my interests.'

'Maybe lack of compromise on both sides.'

'I believed I didn't count so I stopped attending anything sporty and made a life on my own.'

He scooted along the cushions, stopping inches from her knees. His fingers caressed her neck and tangled into her hair.

'You count, Lauren, in every way that matters.'

'I know that now, just not sure how much with them.'

She suddenly hit him, flat-handed over his heart, making him jerk away.

'Admit it, Matt Dalton, you were one of those guys like my brothers, who assumed being athletic made you better than those who weren't. And more deserving of attention from girls.'

Matt's fingers stilled, his stomach clenched. She'd nailed him. Major benefits of being in the school's A-grade had been the accolades, the admiration of lesser-gifted pupils. The chicks he could take his pick from.

Hell, that sounded egotistical.

'And I'll bet you barely noticed anyone who wasn't beautiful, confident and out there.' Her jaw lifted and one finger tapped on his chest. Her hazel eyes flashed with challenge.

'Ah, but I did.' He grinned at her defiance. 'I was nineteen, surrounded by adoring girls yet I followed a shy, unknown escapee into the dark and kissed her. She ran and I ended up going home alone because I couldn't find her again.'

'You didn't?'

She doubted his word. Understandable maybe but it irked. He prided himself on his honesty. Taking her drink, he plonked it on the table heedless of the splashing droplets. He bent forward, splaying his hand on the lounge arm, enclosing her and forcing her to lean away.

'You don't believe me? How can I persuade you it's true?'

'You can't.' Proud and playfully stated.

She had no idea how provocative she looked arched over the armrest, enticing full lips parted and bold eyes sparking.

Or did she? The tapping stopped. Pity, he'd liked it from her. She sucked in a deep breath, her head tilted and wariness drove defiance from bright hazel.

Ashamed of his brash behaviour, he shifted but kept within reach. Picking up the glasses and holding hers out, he noticed the motion of the wine. *From his trembling.* He drained the remainder of his, shaken by his reaction.

'Forgive me. I said tonight was for talking. I won't make that promise for the future though. There's something between us, Lauren, something too strong to ignore.'

'It'll pass. There'll be other women in your life.'

'You're the only one now. It's you I want.'

Her head swung from side to side in slow motion as if that would change his statement. He halted the movement by cupping her chin.

'I don't lie, Lauren. And I can wait until you're ready to admit it too. In the meantime, we could call Alan, who'll confirm my story. I shared a cab with him and his date.'

She flicked him a half-smile. 'No phones tonight, remember.'

Almost an admission she believed him. He feigned an affronted air.

'You questioned my word. I deem that an emergency.'

Her instant laughter hit a spot deep inside, denting the armour he'd placed around his heart. Scaring the hell out of him. He'd sworn never to be vulnerable again.

'So why Sydney?' Out of the blue to give him recovery time.

'I was offered a challenging position interstate from Melbourne.'

'A long way from your family.'

'I didn't disown them. I keep in touch, visit reasonably regularly, and always see them when they come to Sydney for a sporting fixture.' She spoke defensively as if she'd heard censure in his voice.

'Which you don't attend.'

'No. They seem to have accepted I'm different. I'm hoping they give this new consideration to their grandchildren.'

'My eldest nephew loves anything involving kicking or hitting a ball, the younger one can take or leave it. We're trying to keep it all fun for as long as possible.'

'There's only the two?'

'Alex and Drew.' He recalled Lena's expression when she'd told him she was pregnant, felt the same rush of affection he'd had then. 'Lena and Mark would love a little girl as well.'

'I wish them success. What did you do in London?'

CHAPTER ELEVEN

STUPIDLY BECAME INVOLVED with a scheming adulteress. Confused physical idolisation with love and almost got sucked into a nightmare.

'I'm a partner in a consultancy firm. We tailor business strategies, give advice and bring investors and companies together. Unlike my father, we don't invest in them though I do have my own portfolio. And I'm very good at what I do.'

She looked away, tightened the hold on her glass, and seemed to shrink in front of his eyes. He thought through his statement, trying to pinpoint what might have upset her.

It hit him like a hammer to his gut, almost overridden by the elation that flooded him. The present tense, still committed. Planning to return.

His heart flipped and his pulse raced. Had she already thought about making love with him and now believed she'd end up hurt if they became involved? It didn't have to be that way if they were completely open and honest. If they didn't let emotion rule their heads, they'd have no regrets when it was over.

He fought the urge to reach for her, draw her into his arms, and tell her that was how it would be. She wasn't ready for such a declaration yet.

'I haven't changed my status as a partner because of the uncertainty. The best scenario would be to get everything legal at Dalton Corporation, and any due taxes paid. I'll get the new project running then I can decide on my future.'

Her sceptical gaze met his. Somehow he had to convince her he was telling the truth, that his main objective was to make the company strong and viable. He hadn't allowed himself to think beyond that.

'Legal proceedings allowing, I'll try to use the same procedure we have in London with Dad's clients, making them independent. The project with Duncan is different, a change of direction for me, but it will stabilise Dalton Corporation.'

Her body had inched forward as if drawn by a magnet. Now the only movement was the slow rise and fall of her chest. Her eyes didn't waver from his.

'It sounds long term.' Husky with a hint of hope. Dared he wish too?

'Anyone's guess. There are too many factors involved.'

Lauren's anticipation deflated. She stared at the glass in her hand, wondering when she'd drunk the remaining wine. From the moment they'd met tonight her emotions had taken her on a loop-the-loop ride, twisting her in knots, ending with a crash landing.

The agenda he'd described would take time and

effort. He'd shrugged it off as no big deal, easily done. Then Europe and his partnership would beckon and he'd go with no looking back. And while he might caress and cajole, he'd never pressure her against her will.

She just wished she could decide what she wanted most.

'Your glass is empty.'

His fingers brushed hers as he took it and she trembled. Something fiery flared in his eyes.

'Would you like a hot drink?'

'No, thank you.' She snuck a glance at her watch as he turned away, torn between wanting to stay and having space to fortify her defences against his charm.

'Hinting it's time to go home?' The laughter in his husky voice teased, and she dipped her head to hide the inevitable blush.

He shuffled closer, avoiding contact, the glasses clinking in his hand, and waited silently for her to raise her head. And the funfair ride took off again at his tender expression. Her stomach flipped, her heartbeat pounded and, she wasn't exactly sure but…had her toes curled? Without even a touch.

'Your choice, Lauren. I'll call a taxi if you want to.'

'Taxi?' Sending her home alone. Shortest funfair ride ever.

'I haven't long finished the second wine. We'll

take a taxi now or have coffee and wait a little longer. I don't take chances when I drive.'

A cosy trip in the back seat or more disclosures here?

'Make mine weak white. Do you need help?'

He only had big mugs so hers wasn't full. It was rich and sweet, complementing the meal. She sipped and enjoyed, noticed he took fewer, bigger swallows.

'Sydney's an expensive city to live in too. Do you live alone or share?'

His polite words were belied by the set of his shoulders, the slight tilt of his head and the heat in his midnight-blue eyes. There'd been no necessity to say he wanted her. Every look, every touch proved he did.

Did she give out the same signals? Her curiosity about him was all consuming yet he'd managed to avoid revealing much personal information.

'Three friends and I put in a bid for one floor of an unbuilt apartment block. One of them is in banking and arranged the mortgages. We got a special price and an input into the layouts and décor.'

'And?'

And what? The other half of his question. He was fishing about her private life.

'I live alone. The other three have partners so it's rare there's not someone around. What about you?'

He ran his hand up her arm creating electrical zings on her skin. All over her skin. He faced her full on, his shoulder pressing into the leather back of the lounge, his arm flat along the top. His fingertips played with her hair.

'Occasionally I have guests.' His face darkened for a second as if remembering an unpleasant experience. 'Not for a while.'

Matt brushed away the past, trying to concentrate on the now. She lived alone, she was single. There was no one who'd have cause to feel offended if he kissed her again.

A companionable silence settled. He gazed into his empty mug, multiple questions racing through his mind, each one too personal to ask unless he intended to make a move tonight. Common sense said it was too soon, they knew little about each other, needed time to build trust. However, would he ever fully trust a woman again?

His libido said he knew all he needed. He wanted her and he'd bet whatever part of the London flat he owned that she wanted him too.

A movement in the corner of his vision broke his reverie in time to see Lauren try to smother a yawn behind her hand. Guess it wasn't going to be tonight.

'You're tired. What do you have planned for tomorrow?

'I'm picking up a hire car and heading to the Barossa Valley for a couple of days. No schedule, just drive and stop whenever something takes my fancy. I'll book into a local hotel each night.'

Two nights.

Plus almost three days without seeing her.

He straightened, tried to swallow past the lump in his throat, tried to ignore the tight band constricting his lungs.

'You'll be back in Adelaide on Friday?' He had to know. Didn't understand why.

'Will you need me then?'

He choked back his instinctive reply.

'I'll keep in touch. Now I'd better get you home.'

He took her hand, led her to the laundry and reached for the door knob to the garage. His brain urged caution. Every muscle tensed with craving. Every cell in his body clamoured, 'Ask her to stay.'

Lauren wasn't his ex, she was as wary as he was. He saw his knuckles whiten and he let go, slamming his hand onto the wall beside her head.

Her eyes widened, her lips parted and her breasts lifted as she sucked in air. He drew her into his arms, his forehead resting on hers. He heard her bag hit the floor and felt one arm encircle his waist. The other hit his chest between them.

It felt good, so good. But not enough. He ached for something unattainable, something that didn't exist. He'd have to settle for whatever she was prepared to give. For being close and building up memories that wouldn't turn sour in acrimony.

She leant into him, and had to be aware of his harsh breathing, how hard his heart was thumping. How aroused he was.

He bent his head. She lifted hers to meet him. He kissed her gently, using every ounce of restraint he could muster, shuddered as her fingertips pushed up his chest to trace a fiery path over his already heated skin. Her unique aroma stirred him with every breath.

He teased her lips into opening, and tasted sweet coffee, mellow wine and Lauren. Encouraged by her muted sighs, he strengthened his hold, stroking and caressing, binding her to him. Only when his lungs screamed for air did he break the kiss, trailing his lips across her neck.

Her eyes moved under closed lids. Her trembling vibrated through him, or were his tremors affecting her? He willed her to look at him and his heart slammed into his ribcage when she did. Gold specks glittering, her hazel eyes smouldered with desire. She wanted him. Primal macho pride surged through him.

But before he allowed himself to accept what her eyes were offering, that same pride decreed he be totally honest, even if it meant she didn't stay. He pressed her head to his shoulder, not wanting to see her expression change, fighting for a softer way to tell her.

There wasn't one. He watched his breath stir her hair as he forced out the words.

'One thing life's taught me is there's no rose-covered cottage with two dogs and a cat and a happy-ever-after waiting for you to find it. Flowers don't last and having a one true love is as rare as a priceless diamond.'

She made a strangled gasp into his shirt. He cupped her chin, raising her head until their eyes met, and felt a strong urge to take it all back just to see the pain vanish. He couldn't. He wouldn't deceive her.

'I want you, Lauren. I want to make love to you so badly it's driving me crazy. But I won't lie. I don't believe in soulmates and endless romance, I've seen too much anguish caused when others have. However, I do believe in and expect complete fidelity.'

Lauren's heart twisted. Someone *had* hurt him, broken him, making him doubt every other woman he met. She fought for composure. If she gave in to desire, she'd be the one counting the cost.

Her heart didn't care, deeming every moment spent with him worth any pain. There was no yesterday, no tomorrow, only now. There was only Matt Dalton, his skin hot under her hand, his body trembling in sync with hers and his heartbeat pounding against her breast.

She inhaled, drew in ocean spray and aroused male. Wanted, ached for more. All-consuming heat coils spiralled from her core. Her fingers itched to unbutton his shirt and caress the muscles it defined.

'Matt?' A dry whisper, pathetically weak for the powerful emotions controlling her.

Passionate blue eyes darkened, his nostrils flared, his lips parted. Something akin to euphoria swept through her. He was no longer the aloof, self-contained executive of fourteen days ago. This was primal man. And tonight she would be his.

'Lauren. I…' Rough. Grating. Emotional.

She touched one finger to his mouth. 'No promises. No tomorrow. Only us tonight.'

With a triumphant growl, he scooped her up, claiming a conqueror's kiss as he strode towards his room. To that massive bed with its rumpled sheets and pillows sure to smell of ocean waves.

The sudden shudder from head to feet took Matt by surprise. His body resonated with the aftermath of the most intense, satisfying sex of his life. As if they'd been transported to a new dimension where only they existed. Lauren had been his, totally, utterly his from the moment he'd lain beside her, kissing and caressing her, moulding her body to his form.

Tightening his arms around her, he held on, riding out the incredible feeling, wishing he could see her beautiful face and her lovely expressive eyes. There was only the faintest light seeping round the edges of the window blinds, only enough to see shadowy outlines.

She was stroking his chest, threatening to reignite the fire that had consumed them both. His willingness to be engulfed by the flame warred with the suspicion that she didn't realise the fervent effect her gentle action evoked.

He placed his hand over hers, sought and found her lips. Keeping the kiss soft and light, he tried to let her know how he felt, elated yet humble, primal yet emotionally moved.

Her soft sigh motivated action.

'Don't go away.' He went to the ensuite, turned on the light, then left the door ajar, allowing subdued light to spill into the room. Bunching up the pillows, he slid into bed and nestled her tight against his side, her head on his shoulder. Her breath blew across his chest, tickling his skin in the nicest sensation imaginable. Her hand lay over his rapid-beating heart.

He'd never initiated after-sex talks, curtailed them as quickly as possible if his partner did. This new desire to learn all he could about Lauren was unnerving and compulsive, so not him. Confidences led to familiarity, which equated with vulnerability. And that he'd determined never to risk.

He stroked her hair for a moment, pressed a kiss on her forehead.

'Why are you so wary of guys like me? Maybe not me so much any more, but it's there. With Alan too.'

Lauren didn't answer. Her body stiffened, she stared at his chest, and her fingers curled. Idiot, he'd pushed too soon. If he could see her face... hell, he knew what he'd see. Fear. Reluctance.

He'd had no choice but to tell her about his father, had given her no reason to believe she could confide in him.

'There was a woman in London I'd known and dated for quite a while. I liked her a lot, though after I wondered if she'd shown her true self to me at all. We shared mutual interests and friends, got on well and I believed we could have a mutually advantageous marriage. It's surprising how many people settle for that. Love wasn't a factor at all.'

He had no idea why he'd confessed his humiliating experience unless it was to show her she could trust him, that she was different from other women he'd known. His calm, rational approach to the relationship with Christine was worlds away from the mind-blowing emotions Lauren aroused simply by being in the same room.

She stirred as if preparing to pull away. He held on, needing contact, and rushed the end of his embarrassing story.

'Luckily for me I discovered she was also involved with a married man before I proposed. I ended the relationship immediately.'

She raised her head and he was stunned by the honest sympathy in her eyes, not a hint of disapproval for his cold approach to a lifetime commitment. He kissed her, holding back the passion that flared. Having her confide in him was paramount even if he wasn't sure why at the moment.

'We've all done things we regret or had them

done to us. I have no right to judge anyone, Lauren. Will you tell me? Whose actions did you brand me, Alan and umpteen other guys with?'

Her eyes clouded a second before she dropped her gaze.to his throat. She quivered, and sucked in a long breath. Feeling like a louse, he was about to tell her it didn't matter.

Lauren blurted the first words out in a breathy rush then steadied as Matt soothed her back with rhythmic caresses.

'Just after Christmas, the same year you and I…you know… There were often weekend barbecues in our place, crowded, noisy, lots of drinking. My brothers' friends got a kick out of teasing me, and calling me little sister to make me blush and get tongue-tied. To them it was harmless fun. I hated it.'

The almost forgotten feeling of helplessness crashed back, clogging her throat, rendering her speechless. Followed just as suddenly by an empowering sensation. She was no longer a victim. She'd grown and moved on. Hadn't she talked to them at Easter without any childish awkwardness?

'I can see now it was thoughtless but never ill intentioned. If I'd been closer to any of my family I'd have been able to tell them how I felt. Instead I used to spend most of my free time with friends. That night the house was quiet inside when I was dropped off. I didn't see my brother's best friend leaning on the dining room door jamb until he lurched out and grabbed me in a bear hug.'

Matt pushed up against the bedhead, taking her with him. 'Lauren, if you—'

'He mumbled, "You're pretty, *li'l sister*," and kissed me. He stank of beer and sweat and to me it was gross. I remember kicking his shins, breaking free and looking over the top of the stair rail with revulsion. He was slumped against the wall, finishing off his can of beer.'

'And you lumped our kiss on the balcony with that?' His incredibility was tinged with anger.

'No! You were…' In her eagerness to appease him she almost divulged how special his kiss had been, how she'd created fantasies of him over the years.

'Matt, I'm sorry, truly sorry. I let one drunken incident influence my judgement of certain types of good-looking men. From his attitude on the few occasions we've met since, I'm convinced he doesn't remember it at all.'

'Lauren Taylor.'

She recognised the corporate tone from their earliest meetings and squeezed her eyes shut as if that would prevent the coming declaration. He tilted her chin up, coaxing her to look into determined midnight-blue eyes.

'You are very special and I intend to banish every skerrick of that image from your memory. In the best, most personal way possible. And I promise you won't want to run from me.'

His kiss was sweet and tender, and, for her, much too short. Humour glistened in his eyes as he raised his head.

'So you think I'm good-looking? Tell me more.'

CHAPTER TWELVE

THERE WERE FEW vehicles on the roads as Matt drove home after leaving Lauren at her hotel room in the early hours of the morning. Gently nudging her through her door and not following tested his resolve. Pulling it shut to enable him to walk away from her sweet smile, flushed cheeks and slumberous hazel eyes was the hardest action he'd ever taken.

He could still feel her soft lips responding to his in the longest, sweetest goodnight kiss he'd ever had. No holding back. No expectations.

He'd asked her to stay all night but understood her need for distance after their shared confessions and lengthy conversation after. It had been soul-searing for them both. They'd have distance all right, three days, two nights and who knew how many kilometres.

He parked in his garage, switched off the engine and clicked the remote to wind down the roller door. Didn't move. Didn't want to go into that empty unit where her tantalising perfume lingered and her presence was now indelibly implanted into the atmosphere.

Reclining the seat and pushing it back, he lay staring at the roof. New, clean, unmarked, like everything else he owned in Australia. Limbo land. Between the old and the unknown.

He closed his eyes—body weary, mind wide awake. His impulsive kiss so long ago had caused repercussions he'd never have believed, and distress for Lauren. He'd allowed his perception of his parents' relationship to affect his attitude. Love might not be blind but maybe it blurred faults in those you cared for.

Lena and Mark, Duncan and Clair. There were other happy couples he knew too. Did his mother's love override the pain of his father's affairs?

He yawned, ought to go in, get a few hours' sleep to cope with the long day ahead. He'd miss her in his bed—probably lie awake remembering the passion they'd shared. Had those harsh, ecstatic groans of release mingling with her joyful cries come from him? His lips curled, his body shifted as he remembered her kittenish mews. He slept.

Lauren woke early, a faint ray of daylight competing with the street lamps to dispel the night. She quivered as memories teased her from sleep, and grew stronger, more vibrant. More intimate.

She blushed as she recalled how forward she'd been, so unlike the compliant participant in her other relationships. Matt had gently encouraged her, kissed her until she was molten lava in his arms then taken her to the stars and beyond.

It was because of those new and tumultuous sensations, followed by the sharing of their innermost secrets, that she'd asked him to take her back to the hotel. Part of her had longed to stay, to sleep cradled to his body and make love in the morning as the sun rose. The other half had felt vulnerable, shocked by her ardent responses, and needing solitude to decipher why now? Why him?

A similar duel had her torn between knowing how much she'd miss him and feeling an inexplicable inclination to re-erect the defence shield round her heart. She had three days to…who was she kidding? Her surrender had been complete.

Thirteen hours later she pushed her dinner plate to the far corner of the table and opened the green patterned spiral notebook she'd bought in the quirky gift shop a few hours ago. Along with presents for friends' future birthdays.

She'd never been one for writing copious holiday descriptions, relying on photos, brief notes and her memory. She'd kept Matt's image at bay as she drove, forcing her mind into work mode where nothing was allowed to intrude on the task at hand. New vehicle, new roads, though there were fewer freeways than in New South Wales.

As she wrote and sipped delicious rose tea she noticed the small ceramic vases on the dining-room tables, each one unique and holding two fresh flowers and a sprig of greenery. *Her* vase with orchids was swathed in bubble wrap and secured behind the passenger seat of the car.

Laying her new special green pen down, she cradled her cup, recalling his tenderness and sensitivity, and the way his passion, matching hers, had overridden both. No one had ever made her feel so feminine, so aroused. She relived the evening from the initial eye contact across the road to his reluctant expression as he'd closed her hotel-room door.

Lost in reminiscence, she jumped when her mobile rang, rummaged for her phone with unsteady fingers.

'Matt.'

'Hi, having a good day?'

His now oh-so-familiar raspy voice triggered a rush of heat through her veins. She leant her elbow on the table, and pressed her mobile tighter to her ear as if the action would bring them together.

'Yes, I turned off at any interesting sign, and stopped at almost every town I went through. The autumn colours are incredible. I took lots of photos and bought a few presents.' She was babbling, couldn't seem to slow down.

'Did you miss me?' Deeper, hopeful tone.

'If I say yes, you'll claim an advantage. How did your meetings go?

'Chicken. I missed *you*. Only had one. Where are you now?'

She clutched her stomach to quell the fluttering

his confession created, steadied her breathing, and fought for her normal placid tone when she replied.

'Nuriootpa for the night. Tomorrow, who knows?'

'You will be back on Friday?' The teasing note disappeared. He sounded serious, surprisingly uncertain.

'That's the plan. Is there a problem?'

'Not from my end. You'll be getting a call from Clair in the next hour or so. We've been invited to their home in the Hills for the weekend.'

'We?'

'As in you and me, Lauren. Duncan wants to discuss the company's current position, and the business proposal I pitched to him a couple of weeks ago in a relaxed atmosphere. They want you to come with me.'

'Why? I'm not part of your deal at all.'

'They like you.'

Not exactly the answer she wanted to hear.

'Lauren, *I* want you to come. You know them, said you liked them. If it's our relationship worrying you, I promise nothing will happen between us unless you want it to.'

Of course she wanted it to; the location was irrelevant. Last night had been the most wonderful experience of her life. The dilemma was the when and where.

'A whole weekend in someone's home is a giant leap from having dinner with them.' With added pressure if they believed she and Matt were involved.

He made an exasperated noise in his throat.

'I wish I could see you, reassure you. Will you please consider it? Talk it out with Clair?'

She shared the same desire to be with him but she was also aware of how much he was counting on making a deal with Duncan Ford. Would it make a difference if she could see his expression? Moot point so far apart.

'Okay. I'll decide when I talk to Clair.'

'Let me know. Now tell me where you went and what you did.'

Matt almost rolled off the lounge as he lunged for his mobile an hour or so later, failing to stifle a harsh groan as his elbow hit the side of the coffee table, and his mug fell off.

'Lauren.'

'What was that?'

Simultaneous voices, then silence.

'Matt, are you there?' He liked, more than liked, the concern in her tone.

'I knocked my elbow on the table. You can kiss it better on Friday.' He sat on the sofa's edge, ramrod straight, stomach taut.

'Try pawpaw ointment, it works quicker.'

'Not as much fun. Clair phoned?' He held his breath.

'The two of you are very persuasive. She reminded me I offered to have a look at her computer some time, so I could hardly refuse. And she promised it'll be a weekend to remember.'

His commitment as well. He rose to his feet, adrenaline surging, his free hand fisting and pumping the air. Couldn't, didn't want to stop the grin from forming but managed to keep his voice steady.

'It will be. Are you tired?'

'A little. I'm in the motel room ready for bed.'

A vivid image from his bedroom filled his head, he barely managed to stifle the zealous groan.

'Too sleepy to talk? You're a long way away, and I don't want to say goodnight.'

'What about?'

'You and your family. Why you took the job in Sydney.'

He waited as she pondered his question, a habit he'd learnt to expect, professionally and personally.

'What I went through might have been because I was so different, too shy and inhibited to join in boisterous games. My parents and brothers were all extroverts, loved any kind of physical sport and had no problems interacting with strangers.'

A decidedly male growl resonated in Lauren's ear.

'They didn't allow for you being quiet and gentle, didn't make time to understand who you were?'

She sensed Matt's anger, found his defending their lack of sensitivity towards her exhilarating.

'I'm beginning to see how I contributed to the problems. I wasn't interested so I didn't make any effort. I never complained or told them how I felt except to refuse to attend any more sporting events once I turned thirteen. To them I seemed happy to bury myself in books and homework. At least I always got good grades at school.'

Another growl so she quickly added, 'If I hadn't I might not be working with computers. Might not be here.'

'Eighty odd kilometres away. Much too far.'

She snuggled into the pillow, striving to keep grounded. He made her feel warm and light-headed even along a phone line. With each word, her pulse had quickened, electric tingles danced over her skin, and the overwhelming desire to touch him, feel his strength surrounding her was almost frightening. He could make her feel strong, empowered. He could also hurt her more than anyone else in the world.

Lauren returned the hire car early Friday afternoon, and was given a sealed package Matt had left for her containing a key to his unit. Finding a round dining setting in the appropriate place and three large bright blue cushions on the settee left her speechless.

She texted him to say she'd arrived, found a tea towel in a kitchen drawer, and set it on the new table. It was the perfect place for the orchid arrangement he'd sent her. They were as fresh as when she'd received them, having suffered no ill effects from their journey to the Barossa.

A cup of tea, an open packet of chocolate biscuits, and she was ready to sort out her belongings in the lounge room. The items she chose for the Hills visit were packed into the new suitcase she'd purchased, everything else was wrapped and stored in her original one ready for the trip home.

Home. Her own apartment. Her sanctuary. It was never going to feel quite the same. The memories she'd be taking with her would change the way she viewed her life, her work. Her future. She chomped into another biscuit and vowed, no matter what, there'd be no regrets. Her friends would be there for her though she'd never be able to tell them the full truth. Matt would be her special *good* secret, hers alone.

She heard his car pull into the garage, his footsteps in the passage, his delighted raspy tone. 'You're here.' She saw his captivating smile, was swept into his embrace, and held as if she was fragile and precious. She slid her arms around his waist, revelling in his strength and the satisfying sense of security.

His lips feather-brushed her forehead. She cuddled up, wanting this serenity to last, and he seemed in no hurry to end it either. Quiet harmony. An idyllic memory to cherish.

'You kept the orchids?'

She arched her neck to meet questioning eyebrows and curved lips. 'Of course. They're beautiful, Matt.'

His eyes shone as he gathered her in. 'So are you, Lauren. Beautiful and intoxicating.'

His kiss was light, gentle, spreading a warm glow from head to toes. Her lips instinctively moved with his. Her heart soared, and she wanted to freeze-frame this precious moment for ever.

With evident reluctance he eased away.

'If I don't let you go now, we'll arrive in the dark. I know which I'd prefer…'

'But the Fords are expecting us for dinner. I'm packed and ready.'

'Give me ten minutes to shower and change.' He dipped his head for a brief hard kiss and walked out of the room.

When they left Lauren kept silent at first allowing Matt to concentrate on the driving through peak traffic. She stared out of the window, trying to identify the suburbs and buildings, surprised by the number of new houses and renovations on main roads.

Once they hit the freeway to the hills, he turned on the radio, keeping it muted in the background.

'Any listening preference, Lauren?'

'Whatever you usually have on is fine.'

'Which would mainly be news and sport. Not for you. How are you on county and western?'

He had to be teasing. One look at his profile said he wasn't.

'As long as it's ballads and not yippee-ki-yay stuff.'

'Whatever pleases you.' He glanced over and her mouth dried up at the fire in his eyes. She quivered inside at the thought of the two nights and two days ahead.

'I've been meaning to ask you for days, kept forgetting because you have a habit of distracting my mind and scrambling my brain. What's the name of your perfume?'

She couldn't answer, her own brain turning to mush at his compliment. He was claiming to be as affected as she was when they were together. Did he have the same heat rushes, the tingles? The heart flips?

She'd been wearing the same brand for years, had one of the fragrances in her suitcase. So why couldn't she remember either name?

'It's from a small rural company who produce different aromas from Australian native flowers. I keep three and wear whichever suits my mood at the time.'

'It's been the same one every day since you arrived. Are the others as enticing?'

'I've no idea. Why do you always wear the same sea-spray cologne?'

'The truth?'

'Yes.' *Please don't let it be because it was a gift from a girlfriend.*

'I forgot to pack mine for when I changed after a game and borrowed Alan's. Apart from when I've been given others, it's the one I use.'

'You wore it that night.'

'For the first time.' He flicked her an incredulous look. 'You remembered how I smelt?'

'You did get pretty close, Matt.'

'Yeah, and then I lost you.'

They drove in silence for a while, both lost in thoughts of their meeting on the balcony, Matt's focus on the road and Lauren's out of the window.

Because of the long hot summer, the vegetation wasn't as green as she'd hoped. Sneak views of houses between the trees, horses and sheep grazing, and colourful native plants drew her avid attention. Seeing a herd of alpacas in a small fenced area of a paddock thrilled her.

After exiting the freeway, they followed the signs through the small typical hills town and onto a winding, tree-lined road. High overhanging branches covered with autumn leaves of brilliant orange and brown shaded them from the setting sun. The verges were covered with more, tempting walkers to romp through them.

'This is so peaceful. So Australiana. When we lived in the suburbs I used to dream of moving to a hills town. Any one of them.' She shrugged. 'Didn't happen of course.'

Matt pulled over, switched off the engine and unbuckled his seat belt. He stretched his arm and unclipped hers, unfazed by the sudden apprehension in her eyes. Twisting to face her and taking her hands in his, he yearned for the glowing satisfaction he'd seen after they'd made love.

'You had a few unfulfilled childhood wishes, didn't you?'

She shrugged. 'Doesn't everyone?'

'No.' He ignored his ambition to work as a partner with his father. 'Most of mine came true. I played Aussie Rules for the school, graduated from uni and travelled overseas. Considering my lack of vocal ability, becoming an international singing sensation was never going to happen.'

His heart swelled at the sight of her hesitant smile. Give him time and he'd make her radiant and happy.

'I dreamt of being a dancer for a year or so.' She gave a self-conscious laugh. 'Of course, in my imagination I had no fear of appearing on stage in front of hundreds of people. The one time I was selected to read a poem I'd written at parents' night, I took one look at all those faces, froze and bolted.'

'So you wrote?'

'I have a stack of notebooks full of poems and short stories, only ever shown to my best friend.

Childish and not very good but fun. I haven't written anything for years except reports or emails.'

Her fingers gripped his. His pulse accelerated. The temperature in the car rose rapidly.

'I've been reflecting on my life lately and I'm beginning to realise my family and I just didn't gel. Maybe they weren't as much insensitive as bemused by the alien in their midst. And there were no other relatives around who might have made a difference.'

'Will you discuss it with them when you see them?'

'No.' Short and sharp. 'There's no way it wouldn't sound accusing and the past can't be changed.'

He silently agreed with fervour.

'I'm an adult with a good career and great friends. It'll achieve nothing, and only cause pain.'

A car drove past, the driver beeping in customary rural friendship. Matt checked the time, then cradled her face in his hands.

'Most assuredly an adult, Lauren Taylor. Beautiful and desirable.'

He intended the kiss to be gentle, reassuring, but almost lost control when she returned it with enthusiasm. Her hands slid up his chest to tease his neck, heating his blood to near boiling. Her body pressed to his fuelled the urge to have her alone somewhere quiet and private.

He broke away, expelling the air from his lungs,

gasping in more as he feasted on her blushed cheeks and brilliant eyes. His hand shook as he redid his seat belt and started the engine.

As he struggled to find his voice again he mulled over her confessions of the last few days. He needed to know everything if he was to help her completely overcome her insecurities before she left.

Before she left. The very idea depressed him. Having her near lifted his spirits.

'In five hundred metres turn right.'

The GPS interrupted his thinking and he slowed down.

CHAPTER THIRTEEN

LAUREN'S LIPS TINGLED from his kiss, and her heartbeat loped along in an erratic rhythm. She wanted to be alone with Matt, wasn't ready for a whole weekend with comparative strangers who'd probably invited her for his sake. Her first sight of the property increased her reservations.

Well-maintained tall hedges formed the property's boundaries with ornate stone columns and high elaborate gates protecting the entrance. She could see neatly trimmed red-and green-leafed plants skirtinged the winding gravel driveway, and a variety of trees and shrubs hid the house from view.

Matt pressed a button on a matching bollard, answered a disembodied voice and the gates swung open. They passed through, and for Lauren it was like entering another world, where money was no object and the traditions of generations would be strictly upheld. She had no logical reason for the feeling yet it was strong and overwhelming, negating all the assurances Matt and Clair had given her.

She gripped her hands in her lap, drops of sweat slid down her back and her stomach churned. Having lunch in public, with eating and waiter service taking up time, hadn't been as bad as she'd expected. The dinner function had been so noisy, so crowded and bustling, interaction had been kept to a minimum.

She'd been coerced into a weekend with Matt and the Fords, dining with them three times a day, sitting with them in the evening. She'd be alone with Clair while the men discussed business. What did she have in common with a rich, influential woman whose life revolved around her husband, family and society friends?

She… Oh, they'd stopped as the car rounded a curve. Wide expanses of lawn had been laid as a fire break on the sides she could see. Ahead stood the house, a beautiful sprawling example of a colonial family homestead with a shady wide veranda on all four sides. It was painted in muted shades of green and brown, including the shutters, to blend with the surroundings. A peaceful harmonious haven. A millionaire's paradise.

She was vaguely aware of the lack of engine noise, then Matt's hand covering hers, raising the hairs on her skin, triggering warmth deep inside. Somehow it intensified the trembling she tried to hide.

She looked into sympathetic blue eyes and wished she'd been more honest and refused the invitation. So much hung on the impression he made this weekend, and she'd be a liability he'd regret.

'I'm sorry, Matt. I made a mistake. This is a

mistake. The dinner was one thing—this is way bigger. You and Duncan talk business, sport, topical news. You were brought up in the same social environment, probably went to the same private school. I'll never fit in with your elite circles.'

A guttural rumble came from his throat and he placed two fingers on her lips. She swatted them away.

'Clair is a caring, generous person with all the social skills. I'm a computer geek with hardly any. We'll run out of conversation in minutes.'

His features hardened, sending an icy chill shooting across her skin as if she'd entered a supermarket freezer. She pressed into the seat, wishing she could disappear into it.

'Those statements are beneath the person I believe you are, Lauren. They met you and thought you were a charming, intelligent, and gracious young woman. Duncan's exact words when he asked me to thank you for your kindness to Ken. And, believe me, Clair would never have invited you just to make equal numbers.'

He stroked her hair, clasped her nape and gently drew her upright. His gaze intensified as he studied her face. What was he searching for? And why? His smile obliterated her logic and created chaotic fantasies.

'They'd like you to have a relaxing weekend in one of the most beautiful places in South Australia, the same as I do. I'm sure Clair knows we're attracted to each other but there's no way she'll say or do anything to make you feel uncomfortable.'

Shame made her blush and she bit her lip. She gave him a remorseful smile, and flattened out her hands with linked fingers in supplication.

'I guess deep inside I know that's true. Sometimes the insecure child overrides the logical technician. Being with you plays havoc with my rationality.'

Too late she heard what she'd admitted, knew from his smug grin he'd understood, and wouldn't hesitate to use it to coerce and cajole her.

'You've just paid me one of the nicest compliments I've ever had. If I wasn't parked in view from the house, and constrained by my seat belt, I'd put it to the test.'

He covered her lips, teasing and coaxing yet with an underlying restraint. She returned the kiss, safe in the knowledge it could go no further. For now. She wound her arm around his neck to hold him closer then let it slide slowly away when he lifted his head. Embraced the surge of power at the emotion in his voice when he whispered in her ear.

'And don't think for a second I won't remember every word and every touch next time we're alone.'

Bringing her breathing under control as they drove up to the house, she silently echoed his words. Except *she'd* remember them as long as she lived.

* * *

Clair was waiting on the front steps and came out to meet them, leaning into Lauren's window.

'Glad you made it. We've opened one of the garage doors for you round the back. I'll meet you there.' She didn't comment on the five-minute time gap from gate to front door.

They parked and Matt was unloading the boot when she joined them, giving Lauren a warm hug and a kiss on the cheek. So different from the casual greetings from her family. Did her reticence cause the awkwardness between them?

'Do you need a hand with the luggage?'

'She's brought less than any woman I've ever travelled with,' Matt chipped in as he received the same greeting. 'And that includes the carton of wine from the Barossa.'

'Oh, how thoughtful. Let me take your suitcase.'

She led the way to the steps, wheeling Matt's case, accompanied by Lauren with hers and an overnight bag. Matt locked the car and followed carrying the wine, his satchel and parka.

'I've put you in the guest wing, three bedrooms all with an ensuite, a sitting room and small kitchen. Completely self-contained if needed.'

As they stepped onto the veranda two black and white dogs raised themselves from their snug positions in the corner and came over to sniff and be introduced. The larger one, a mixture of collie and a few unknowns, nuzzled at Lauren's hands and she dropped her bags and stroked him. The other sat by Clair and studied the two newcomers.

'Cyber's an addict for attention. He'll stalk you the whole time you're here if we let him. Cyan is pure collie, and quieter. Both are very protective and great guard dogs. Go settle, you two.'

Turning to the right, she walked a few steps and opened a door to reveal a wide corridor with a high ceiling. Entering first, she placed the suitcase by the wall.

Lauren's eyes widened at the incredible décor, presumably historically accurate with the appearance of being freshly painted in shades of blue. She'd always enjoyed colonial movies, now she felt she was on the set of one. The carved wooden mirror on the wall with a narrow matching table fascinated her. She moved closer. Clair came to stand behind her.

'We inherited these and a lot more furniture with the house. Tomorrow I'll take you on a tour if you like.'

'I'll look forward to it.'

'You'll find we've mixed and matched different time periods. If we like it, we fit it in. Use any rooms you want and join us in the main lounge when you're ready. Shall I take the wine?'

'It's heavy so I'll bring it. We won't keep you waiting.' Matt had already put it on the floor.

'I just need a quick freshen up,' Lauren said.

'Take all the time you want, then come through

here.' Clair left through a door midway along the hall.

'Well, Lauren, would you like to choose where you sleep?'

At odds with its rough timbre, his voice glided as smooth as silk over her skin and the only answer in her head was, *With you*.

The first room was a cosy corner lounge with windows on two sides. Matt opened the next door to reveal a king-sized bed with a padded green headboard and quilt. The light green wall complemented white woodwork and built-in wardrobes.

Shuttered windows overlooked the veranda, and the Queen Anne dressing table and stool between two closed doors matched the bedside drawers. One door led into a very modern ensuite, the other to an almost identical bedroom with a floral theme.

Lauren gazed from one to the other then to Matt's inscrutable expression. His taut jaw and the slight curl of his fingers showed the depth of his tension.

She bent her head to hide a smile. If she said separate rooms, he'd accept her decision without censure though she'd bet he'd use his charm and every seduction technique he could think of to change her mind.

Her stomach quivered and she trembled as she imagined a few of them. In an instant, he was holding her arms, sombre eyes scanning her face.

'Whatever feels right for you, Lauren. This is for happy memories, no regrets.'

She reached up to caress his cheek, and felt his tremor through her fingers. Felt a surge of elation at the power her touch had on him. She tilted her head, and curled her lips in what she hoped was a beguiling smile.

'I've never been a flowery décor girl, and I can't imagine *you* sleeping under a floral quilt.'

His smile lit up her world, his bear hug squeezed her ribcage, and his deep, passionate kiss had her craving to be in the bed behind them right now.

Lauren expected dinner to be in a formal room. Instead the round dining setting overlooked a native garden scattered with inconspicuous bollard lights, illuminating colourful flowers and leafage of all shades of green. Picture perfect scenery.

Duncan opened a red wine she'd purchased in the Barossa Valley and one of his own chilled whites.

'Lauren, which would you like? We are firm advocates for indulging in your own preference.'

She chose white, the others elected to try the red. They toasted good friends and she was complimented on her choice, making her relax and laugh.

'I can hardly claim responsibility. Matt recommended two of the wineries and I merely asked the people in those, and a third near Angaston, for a selection of their bestsellers. It's a gift from both of us.'

'Very much appreciated. Shall we take our seats?'

Clair went to fetch the starters, declining Lauren's offer to assist.

'They're all ready to be served. You can help clear and bring in the other courses.'

Any apprehension Matt had felt regarding this visit faded away as conversation flowed. Lauren was curious about the plant varieties in the garden, admitting she'd had a successful vegetable plot in Melbourne and missed the straight-from-the-ground taste. When laughingly challenged by Clair to name the home-grown on the table, she amazed them all by being correct.

'I thought I'd get you on the peas from the market. We'll pick some fruit for you to take home on Sunday.'

The conversation ranged from orchards to the history of the house and the restorations the Fords had undertaken over a number of years. Matt admired the gentle banter between them, the friendly teasing solidly based on an enduring love and evident companionship.

He'd been convinced he'd never feel such a bonding, yet lately that belief had become blurred. Was it possible he might be wrong?

His eyes met Lauren's as she stood to help with the dinner plates, and her smile tripped his heart.

His mind flashed to the night ahead with the enchanting woman who'd agreed to share it with him.

Pavlova, coffee and liqueurs rounded off a delightful meal, his senses heightened by the promise of a perfect ending to the day.

All Lauren's senses were acute, tuned like a maestro's violin, as they approached the door that would shut them off from the rest of the house. Matt's fingers were laced with hers. She could hear the long breaths he took. His aroma surrounded her, tempting her lungs to breathe deeper.

Tonight there'd be no drive back to her hotel. She'd nestle into his warmth and fall asleep. And wake in his arms to be kissed and loved some more as the sun's rays lit up the room.

No expectations. No recriminations. She'd accept what he freely gave and not regret what he was not able to give. Every moment spent with Matt inched her further along the path of surrendering her heart. There was no going back and in front she could see no happy ending.

As soon as the door closed behind them, he twisted her round, and stepped closer, trapping her against the wall. He stroked her cheek with his knuckles, and she could feel his heart pounding under her palm. His free hand slid around her neck and he bent his head to claim her lips.

The fire that had smouldered since he'd arrived home roared into flame, and she returned his kiss with an ardour that shook her to her core. He quivered then his arms enfolded her, tightening until there was no space between them.

Time stood still, stretched endlessly to infinity. Too short an eon later, he raised his head to take a shuddering breath. Her own came in gasps, and she let her forehead rest on his chest.

'Wow.' Placing one hand on the wall above her head, he blew air out and inhaled new in. Stared at her for a long time as if trying to see inside her head, trying to puzzle something out.

'I've missed you, Lauren. Ached for you for three long days and two endless nights and I can't wait any longer.'

He lifted her into his arms, carried her into the bedroom, and laid her on the bed. Without relinquishing hold, he settled beside her, rolling onto his side to lean over her. His fingertips skimmed across her shoulders and arms then over her hips, making her squirm with anticipation. His lips kissed a path from the pulse by her ear to the corner of her mouth, driving her crazy with need.

'Matt?' She hardly recognised the breathless, needy plea as coming from her. Her hand pressed on the back of his neck, dragging his head down to hers, and her fingernails scraped his skin.

'You're mine.' His voice was harsh, deep with passion. Macho. Triumphant.

'Yours.' Hers was breathless. Elated. Proud.

For as long as he needed and wanted her.

* * *

Lauren leant on the veranda rail waiting while Matt showered so they could join their hosts for breakfast. The universe was different, sharper, brighter. *She* was different.

She huffed and watched her breath evaporate in the cool air. She'd been changing since Matt had glanced up at her with his mesmerising midnight-blue eyes. A little every time they were together, stronger from the kisses outside her hotel room and a giant leap when they first made love.

Last night the metamorphosis had become complete. There'd been no sign of the shy, vulnerable caterpillar. She'd given herself to him completely, no hesitation, no restraint. And been shown a realm of soaring passions and sensations far beyond her imagination.

She'd fallen into contented sleep wrapped in his arms, his lips on her forehead, her hand on his thundering heart.

She felt a nudge at her side, and hunkered down to pat Cyan, almost fell over as Cyber also claimed attention.

'Save some for me.' Matt stood in the doorway, hair damp, eyes gleaming.

He could have all of her for as long as he wanted.

Breakfast was served on the balcony facing the large vegetable patch. Lauren loved the crispness in the air, and the light breeze stirring the foliage, making the garden appear to be alive. She could imagine sitting here all day and into the evening enjoying the changes of light and sound.

'This is all so idealistic. I can't imagine a more soothing place. Working in the city must be so much more tolerable if you know you have a haven to go home to.'

'And work's better now I can do a lot electronically,' Duncan chipped in. 'You can keep your high-rise views. Nothing beats what we have here.'

'Do you get out of the city much, Lauren?' Clair asked as she buttered her toast.

'Occasionally. We drive up to the Blue Mountains or along the coast to go hiking. Beach walking is fun any season and easily accessible in Sydney.'

'And who's we?'

Lauren noted she gave no apologies for being inquisitive, didn't need to. It was part of her caring nature.

'A group of friends I've met since moving there. We now live in the same apartment block so we're like family.'

As she spoke she looked across the table at Matt's thoughtful expression, remembered earlier conversations and wondered if he'd come to the same sudden realisation. She had a second family, of her own ilk, and who she gelled with comfortably.

He quirked an eyebrow and his lips curled, causing fluttering in her belly and heat waves in her veins. She lifted her glass, drank the remainder of her freshly squeezed orange juice, and tried for a nonchalant demeanour.

CHAPTER FOURTEEN

MATT STRUGGLED FOR the same effect. His body still buzzed from the exhilaration of waking from deep satisfying sleep with Lauren curled into him, warm and irresistible. He had no idea what he'd eaten, drunk or said since they'd joined Duncan and Clair for the meal.

She was radiant. Her skin glowed and her expressive hazel eyes shone as brightly as any stars in a country sky. He'd heard and understood what she'd said. She had friends and support. She'd be all right when she went home.

Home. His half-empty barren unit. She'd taken three days of her leave. Allowing for the day or two he'd need her at work, she'd only be here for two more weeks. Forget the hotel. He'd ask her to stay with him.

The prospect of spending long evenings with her was intoxicating. The image of her sharing breakfast and dinner across the new table he'd bought because of her upped his pulse to uncountable. And as for the nights...

'Matt?'

He crashed to earth with a thud. Clair's eyes twinkled as she held up the coffee jug.

'More coffee?'

'Um… Please.' He pushed his cup and saucer over to her, hoping his face wasn't as red as it felt. She'd caught him out again.

'As you two will be in Duncan's study for most of the morning, Lauren and I will walk the dogs then I'll show her over the house,' Clair said, topping up her husband's drink.

'Just don't let her get you in the small room off the lounge, Lauren,' Duncan quipped. 'That's where her troublesome computer lurks and you'll be trapped in there until dinner.'

'Brute.' Clair gave him a playful flick of her hand and they smiled blissfully at each other.

The painful gut wrench took Matt by surprise. Their affection was obvious after nearly thirty-five years of marriage. Duncan had mentioned their anniversary was in June and he intended to make it an extra special occasion.

He'd assumed it would be for show like his parents' celebrations. Not any more. Like Lena and Mark, the interaction between them proved their feelings ran deep and true.

The dogs bounded down the back steps as soon as Lauren and Clair came out of the door, raced halfway across the lawn then stopped to ensure they were following.

'They're better than any exercise programme I've ever tried,' Clair remarked. As the two women caught up with them, they shot off again.

'Walking anywhere around here would never seem like training to me. This trip has got me re-thinking my priorities and future,' Lauren replied.

'The trip or the man?'

Lauren wasn't sure how to answer as they went through a gate and onto a bushland path.

'It's complicated.'

'It needn't be, Lauren. The way you look at one another, whenever you touch, the attraction's obvious but there's also constraint. My children tell me not to interfere...'

'Advice is always welcome.' Lauren would gladly accept guidance. 'It's whether it can be acted upon that counts.'

'Don't give up on him, Lauren. Matt's mother and I belong to the same organisations, and she's hinted at Marcus's medical problems. Apart from that and the company situation, I sense Matt has personal demons to conquer.'

'You may be right.'

He's certainly determined to have me exorcise mine.

'He also has a reputation for tough, ethical dealing. If he didn't Duncan wouldn't be considering a partnership. Let him find his own way and be there when he does.'

As things stood she'd be on the east coast fixing glitches, living on memories and dreaming of midnight-blue eyes.

'Cyber. Cyan.' The dogs had darted to the left at a fork, and obediently returned to Clair's side.

'There's a magnificent view this way. Luckily the koalas don't seem at all perturbed by our noisy pets so keep an eye out for them in the gum trees.'

'I envy you all this beauty and peace. Matt told me the property was quite run-down when you moved in.'

'I inherited the estate from two wonderful stubborn-as-mules grandparents who refused help and died within weeks of each other. Life wasn't easy, especially in those early years, but it's always worth fighting for what you love.'

But what if the one you are fighting for doesn't want to be won?

The talks with Duncan couldn't have gone better; now all Matt wanted to do was find Lauren, and see her smile. Had she had a good morning? Was she happy she'd come?

He found her in the kitchen helping Clair prepare a salad lunch, and restrained the desire to kiss her in company. Until her face brightened at the sight of him and the invitation in her bright eyes was too hard to resist. He slipped his arm around her waist and softly covered her enticing lips with his.

She laid her hand on his arm, and welcomed the kiss, recreating the heat sensations from last night. His pulse tripled and his heart pounded. All overridden by an unfamiliar longing to hold on for ever and cherish.

Shaken by this new emotion, he broke the kiss, fighting for control. He wanted to find solitude to assess what was happening, and perversely ached to scoop her up and carry her to a quiet place and be with her.

'How'd the walk go?' Reality slammed home at Duncan's remark from the doorway.

Matt set Lauren free, nearly pulled her back in at the sight of her sweetly bemused expression.

'The air was fresh and crisp at the south lookout and the hills were shrouded in mist—very bracing,' Clair replied. 'You two can carry the salad bowls and meat plates. Lauren and I will bring the rest.'

The dogs padded round the veranda to join them, squatting close in anticipation of being fed as well.

'We also had a session on my computer,' Clair announced with pride as they helped themselves to food.

'And?'

Duncan wasn't merely playing lip service to his wife. Matt heard the genuine interest in his tone, saw it in his eyes. She was his number one priority as he was hers. So different from his parents. A cold fist crushed his heart, and his chest tightened.

'I'm not so bad after all. Lauren gave me a beautifully covered notebook and bright green pen and I wrote down everything step by step as she told or showed me.'

Lauren's knee bumped against his and stayed. A simple nod of her head plus a look that said 'you were right' sent heat surging throughout his body. He echoed her action then concentrated on Clair.

'No one's ever explained the things I have trouble with in simple English I can understand. Lauren did, and I have her email address and phone number so I can contact her any time I need help.'

Matt couldn't prevent the swell of pride even though all he'd done was persuade Lauren to come. With a start, he realised it was pride in her, something he had no justification for. She was her own person. An enchanting, self-sufficient woman.

'So I'm going to take her into Hahndorf this afternoon. What do you have planned?'

The men exchanged glances.

'Another couple of hours and we'll break for the day. You'll find us on the side veranda with a bottle of wine and a selection of cheese and crackers.' Duncan grinned at Matt. 'They'll have to come get us to carry all the shopping from the car.'

Clearing the table was accomplished in a few minutes with everyone helping then Matt went with Lauren to fetch her coat and shoulder bag. And to kiss her, longer and deeper than he'd be able to do in front of their hosts.

It left them both hot and gasping for air. And bedtime was a lifetime away.

'Glad you decided to come, Lauren?' He watched her face for any sign of regret.

'Got coerced you mean. Yes, I'm very glad.' Her eyes darkened, highlighting the gold flecks. His body responded to the thought she might be re-membering last night.

'Clair says she'll take me round the house to-morrow.'

He'd been in umpteen old renovated homes. A few days ago he'd have politely declined joining them. Today the chance of seeing what the Fords had achieved through Lauren's eyes was appeal-ing.

'Tell her I'd like to be included.'

His wanting to join them delighted Lauren. When the offer of two weeks' leave had been made it had sounded like ample time for a break. Now, with three days taken, it was a pitiful amount to store memories to last a lifetime.

Lauren flicked at the insect biting her earlobe, sighed and snuggled into her pillow. It returned, pulling her a little further from sleep.

'Wanna go for a walk and watch the sun rise?'

Whispered throaty seduction.

In an instant she was wide awake, catching at the hand whose fingernails were tickling her lobe. Matt lay beside her, fully dressed in jeans and warm jumper, eyes gleaming with mischief. The only light came from the open ensuite door.

How come he wanted to go hiking and her main desire was to drag him close for a repeat of last night? And later. And some time in the early hours of today. It would take only his touch to turn her languid muscles molten and rekindle the passion he'd ignited again and again.

'What time is it?' She stretched, and shivered as the cold morning air hit her arms, glared at him when he pulled the quilt off her. He sucked air between his teeth as she tried to drag them back.

'Early. I've got snacks, drinks and directions to the best lookout.' He was excited, eager like a puppy ready for his daily walk. 'You've got five minutes.'

'You asked for ten on Friday,' she muttered, pretending to be annoyed. Secretly she was thrilled he wanted to share this outing with her. His laughter followed her to the shower.

He took her hand as they left, guiding her down the back steps and over the lawn, his torch lighting their way. They followed the path through the trees, accompanied by only the sound of the breeze rustling the vegetation, the scuffling of animals in the undergrowth, and dried leaves crunching under their sneakers.

Lauren relished the chill on her face, the night hiding the factual mundane world and the warmth of his fingers linked with hers. This was more than special, this was super memorable. A never-to-be-forgotten occasion to be taken out and savoured in the future whenever she felt sad.

Matt stopped suddenly in the centre of a small

clearing, and bent to place his backpack on the
ground. She heard a click and the beam disappeared, leaving them in complete darkness, surrounded by black velvet. Magical. Ethereal.

He drew her into his arms, and she wrapped hers
around his neck. His lips were soft, his kiss firm
yet holding a tenderness that touched her heart. No
bells or fireworks. This was a moment of profound
contentment. The moment she acknowledged the
truth. She was in love with Matt Dalton.

With their lips a whisper apart Matt breathed
out Lauren's name, too stunned to form any other
words. He'd switched off the torch for effect, to
heighten the ambiance when he'd kissed her in the
dark. Hadn't expected to be so unsettled by his
own emotions.

Only she could access his soul and revitalise the
beliefs he'd long discarded, make him yearn for
a better time when he'd had faith in for ever. She
fitted him perfectly, her soft form to his hard muscle. He didn't want to—couldn't—let her leave
until he...he wasn't sure what.

Keeping one arm around her as much for his
comfort as hers, he bent to retrieve the torch, waved
it round and led her to the gap in the trees. In the
light's limited sphere there was a valley below and
hills beyond, vague mysterious shapes. The wind
was stronger here in the open, blowing up and over
the edge, causing him to strengthen his stance.

His intention had been to give Lauren a weekend of pleasurable memories. Now he was storing them up for himself.

Taking the picnic rug from the rucksack, he laid it out between the trees near the edge of the cliff. Lying down on one elbow, he held out his hand. His already racing heartbeat hit rocket speed as, without hesitation, she joined him, eyes sparkling, lips parted. She stroked his cheek, and ran her fingers across his jaw, triggering reactions that blew his control.

Shy, exquisite Lauren was teasing him, playing havoc with his libido. She tempted him with her inviting smile, her tongue-tip tracing her lips, and her feather-light finger touch. He bent over her, lowered his head and clicked off the torch.

The first small pink and orange rays shimmered on the horizon. Matt leant against a tree trunk, nestled Lauren's back onto his chest, and rested his chin on her shoulder as they stared across the valley. He breathed in her delicate scent, tinged with his cologne and their personal aromas.

This was an extraordinary moment, life changing. For those few incredible minutes, they'd been one entity, bound by a force he didn't understand. Knew he wanted to relive it again and again.

For ever? She wriggled, reigniting the desire. His body would willingly comply for as long as he lived. His resolute mind clung to the hard lessons he'd learnt. He refused to make false declarations to gain any advantage or to give false hope of any kind.

No deception. No lies. What they had was good, much better than good. There was no reason they couldn't continue to be together until she flew home. His arms tightened, reinforcing his hold, and she gave a cute gasp. He nuzzled her neck and she sighed. He nibbled her earlobe.

'Oh-h-h…' Her breath whooshed out as vibrant colours tinted the edges of emerging clouds and gradually spread across the sky. Dark shadowy shapes began to appear on the landscape, slowly taking recognisable form. Unforgettable. Unbelievably spectacular.

His own breath caught in his throat. His body stilled, his pulse raced. This was supposed to be a unique experience for Lauren to treasure, along with the other special occasions they'd shared. He hadn't expected to feel anything more than he did at fireworks displays or the like.

Instead nature at her finest tugged at his heartstrings, and raised the hairs on the back of his neck. The adrenaline rush was greater than when he'd skied the Swiss Alps and white-water rafted in Wales, heightened by sharing it with Lauren.

The sun's softer morning rays revealed the delicacy of her skin, rapture in her wide-open eyes, and ecstasy on her beautiful face. He burned it into his memory, to be recalled at will.

'Matt.' Husky with emotion. Crumbling what little composure he had left.

'Darling Lauren.' Rough, dragged over the constricting lump in his throat.

'It's wonderful. Unbelievable. Thank you.'

He cradled her cheek, leant forward and kissed her, wishing the earth would stop spinning and the magic would never end. He laid his head next to hers and pretended it hadn't.

Lauren wished she could reverse time, have the sun set then rise again. In slow motion. With her senses already heightened by his gentle loving only minutes before, she'd been enthralled by the fluid change of colours. The panorama in front of her, the solid wall of his chest behind her, and his muscular arms enfolding her intensified the sensation of being snugly cosseted in a vast open universe.

She loved the mystical atmosphere of night becoming day, of small pockets of mist among the trees. Of feeling they were alone in the cosmos. Even the nocturnal creatures were silent in mutual reverence.

His kiss was magical, soft with an underlying hint of yearning. A longing echoed in her heart. A craving for this never to end.

Lights flickered in the distance, and the wind picked up, bringing with it faint sounds of traffic. They ate the chocolate bars and drank the hot coffee he'd brought. Cuddled close in their padded winter jackets, neither ready to leave and return to the real world.

Only when they heard the dogs barking did they stand and pack up.

'I think I need a bigger car,' Matt joked as he juggled the luggage into the boot for the late-afternoon return to the city.

'Don't whinge. I'm the one who'll be paying for excess weight on the plane.' Lauren's light retort masked the pain of knowing every moment brought her departure closer.

They'd have a few evenings, maybe part of the weekends together, and distant phone calls while she was driving around being a tourist. All too soon she'd have used up her ten days and they'd say goodbye.

There hadn't been, nor would there be, any promises or declarations of keeping in touch. And she'd never ask for them.

'It might be cheaper for me to drive you home.'

CHAPTER FIFTEEN

HER HEARTBEAT SPIKED. His tone was light but his eyes were grave, his lips firm and unsmiling. She couldn't have replied to save her life, and ached to have him add he meant it.

'Got room for more?' Clair came down the steps carrying a huge bunch of flowers. 'Duncan's bringing the fruit we promised.'

Lauren pressed her hands together, her index fingertips on her lips. How had she ever been daunted by this considerate, generous couple?

'They're beautiful, Clair. Thank you for a wonderful weekend. It's been unforgettable.'

She recognised roses and tiger lilies, others were unknown. When she reached up to kiss Clair's cheek as she accepted the stunning gift, she was drawn into an unexpected motherly hug.

'You'll always be welcome, Lauren,' Clair said, and gave her an extra squeeze.

'Even when she hasn't stuffed up on her computer.' Duncan laughed as he appeared behind her with a big cardboard box. 'Should last you a few days,' he added, handing it to Matt.

Lauren buried her face into the blooms and inhaled their perfume before placing them on the back seat alongside her overnight bag. Gently touched the petals, blinking back tears at the Fords' kindness.

She noticed Matt and Clair in close conversation, serious expressions on their faces. Was he also being given friendly advice? She walked over to Duncan to thank him and was pulled into a friendly embrace.

'I'll be eternally grateful to you for helping Clair and boosting her esteem. Other technicians made her feel inadequate though she hid it well.'

'It wasn't much compared to your company and hospitality. I've loved every moment.'

'Then come again—plan for a holiday in the spring or in December. Despite the heat, we always have a festive season, including long evening walks followed by hot or cold drinks on the veranda.'

'It sounds inviting.'

'Then be here.' He smiled down at her. 'Pity you're based in Sydney. It's such a long way away.'

The farewells lasted another ten minutes and included more hugs for Lauren as if they feared they wouldn't see her for a long time. Finally they were on the road, and she let her head fall back and closed her eyes.

'Tired, darling?'

Every cell in her body sprang to high alert at his endearment, the second time he'd used it. Was it an automatic name for the women he made love to?

'A little. It's been a full weekend.'

'Any regrets, Lauren?' Low, and slightly hesitant. Not like him at all.

'None, Matt.' She paused and grinned. 'Well, maybe the purchase of a T-shirt depicting a joey in its mother's pouch, waving an Australian flag. I'll give it to a friend with quirky taste.'

Matt chuckled. His mood lifted. The idea he'd been contemplating was the best option for both of them. All he had to do was find the words to convince her. In his usual competent way, he rehearsed the phrasing, while negotiating the bends and merging onto the freeway. Lauren was lost in her own thoughts.

Satisfied he was ready, he glanced across and forgot it all in a rush of affection when he saw her lovely features relaxed in peaceful sleep. He faced the road again, tightening his grip on the wheel to conquer the urge to caress her cheek.

He had the rest of the day for gentle persuasion. If she agreed they'd spend all their free time together for the two weeks she had left. Fourteen days, and he'd count down every one.

Moving into the left lane, he slowed down. There was no urgency, Lauren was peaceful and the hectic uncertainty had eased from his life. He didn't know exactly what he faced legally but he'd been totally honest and had good representation. He had no idea how bad the backlash might be if, more like when, his father's duplicity became public but was assured of Duncan's full support.

He had faith in his own ability to reform the company and keep it viable. And—he shot an affectionate look at his sleeping passenger—he had Lauren. Sweet, adorable Lauren, who hijacked his thoughts at inopportune moments and flipped his heart with a wisp of a smile. She even had him questioning his steadfast beliefs.

A semi-trailer whooshed past in the next lane, too close, causing him to veer to the left. Lauren stirred and stretched her back, blinked and gave him an apologetic smile.

'I fell asleep.'

'I noticed. Sweet dreams?'

'I can't remember. Why?'

'You sighed a couple of times, low and contented. Cancel the hotel booking, Lauren. Stay with me.' Blunt and rushed—not as he'd practised. 'Sorry, I had a persuasive speech planned. Logical reasons to...'

He stopped midsentence as she silently bent, took her mobile from her bag and scrolled for the number. He shook his head to clear his muddled brain and closed his open mouth. Elation zapped along his veins. She'd be there to welcome him in the evenings. They'd have quiet hours to talk and long nights to hold each other.

'Done. I can do one-day trips to the southern area or the hills.' She dropped her phone into the drinks holder.

They were approaching the turn-off sign and he

checked his rear-vision mirror in preparation for switching lanes. Pulling up at the lights, he covered her hand and revelled in the heat surge that simple act generated.

'And be home for dinner?'

'Oh, if you're expecting meals like Clair served us, you'll be disappointed. I'm very basic, usually cook for one or have cold meat and salad.'

'You've seen my fridge. It's been takeaway or dine out since I arrived home. We'll improvise as we go. I have dinner with my parents on Mondays and call in after work whenever I can.'

'They need your support so that mustn't change. And you can't neglect your sister's family either.'

'I won't. They and Alan are the ones who've kept me grounded and sustained me through it all.'

'You're lucky to have them.'

He flicked her a quick glance. It was a genuine remark with no undertone of acrimony.

'We never tried that pub near the unit. Wanna give it a go tonight?'

Wednesday's dinner was crumbed lamb chops and salad, followed by bakery fruit pie and carton custard. As basic as you could get. Lauren thanked the stars for the local butcher whose selection of ready-to-cook meals was superb and included helpful advice.

She'd revised her plans, exploring Adelaide suburbs and southern coastal areas on alternate days to limit the long drives. Today she'd been to the museum and art gallery in the city, tomorrow's choice was the Fleurieu Peninsula's historic towns.

Their evenings were casual yet special to her. They'd have a quick run of the taped news followed by lively discussions as they watched a favourite programme or two. The nights held mutually shared passion and deep, peaceful sleep.

They lived in the moment. The future was never discussed but she wondered if he thought about it as much as she did.

Anticipation thrummed through her at the sound of his car. Soon she'd have to learn to live without the tingles over her skin, the breathlessness and the tom-tom racing of her pulse.

'Lauren.' She loved his homecoming routine: the same raspy greeting, the same admiration in his midnight-blue eyes, and the deep loving kiss, lasting until the need for air broke them apart. Plus for her the same intense pang to her heart.

'Mmm…' He nuzzled her neck, then sniffed appreciatively. 'Dinner smells almost as good as you. Let's talk 'til it's ready.'

What had happened? Bad news about his father's actions or the company? Serious talking was for as they ate, then forgotten in the pleasures of the evening. The way he grasped her fingers as they sat on the sofa was different, and disturbed her. *He was nervous.*

'What do you have planned for Friday?'

'A tram ride and walk on the beach.'

'Without me?' His eyebrow quirk and sudden grin confused her even more.

'Drive in with me, process the work I need done then go for your walk.'

'And?'

He seemed loath to continue, his eyes dark and intense, trying to predict her reaction to his announcement.

'I've got tickets for the Crows' game in the evening.'

Relief had her sagging into the cushions. That was all? He didn't want to upset her by leaving her alone for a few hours?

'That fine, Matt. It'll do you good to let off steam and I can amuse myself.'

Matt knew damn well she could, how self-reliant she was. While relishing the times she'd depended on him, he also loved her independent spirit. She'd admitted to rethinking her relationship with her family. Now he was hoping Friday's outing would help her move on.

'Two for Alan and his date and one for me.' He paused, eyes on her face. 'The fourth is for you.'

Her reaction was everything he'd hoped for. Wide eyes, gold specks sparkling. Red lips parted and inviting. Index finger pointing at his chest.

'I told you I don't attend matches, only watch bits when I'm visiting friends who have the television on. Take someone else.'

She was magnificent, head high, chin jutted and eyes that flashed defiance. He stored the memory and prepared to counter.

He caught her finger in one hand, and cupped her chin with the other, stroking the silken underside of her stubborn jaw. Inhaled deeply as her eyes softened in response to his action. He so wanted to let her off the hook but it was more important to have her exorcise this demon.

'Lauren, you bound the whole concept of your perceived lack of parental attention with the sports your brothers played. Come and put it to the test. One game. Share a Crows win with me. Supper's on Alan.'

She looked down, bit her lip, and made a flimsy attempt to free her hand. It took little effort for him to hold on. She finally peered up at him and tilted her head.

'Do they still sell hot dogs?'

His heart swelled to bursting point. She was adorable.

'As many as you want, darling.' He pulled her into his arms and if the oven's timer hadn't rung, dinner would have been served a lot later.

Lauren liked Kaye at first sight when she arrived in the office with Alan and pizza. She was a trim, toned extrovert and an avid Crows fan, wearing all the club regalia and waving a beanie at a protesting Matt.

She also had a photo on her mobile screen showing a litter of squirming newborn puppies. A wriggling mixture of brown, white and black.

'You promised to wear it for the rest of the year if I found a suitable puppy for your nephews. These are a cross breed of black Labrador and German shepherd. They'll be gentle and protective, perfect for active children. You get first pick and they'll be ready to take home in five or six weeks.'

'They're adorable. Are you going to let the boys choose?' Lauren enthused, wishing she could have one too. Not practical with her profession or in an apartment.

'Under supervision, otherwise we'll end up with a car full,' Matt insisted, jamming on the hat. He'd cleared his desk for the meal and, when the others went to fetch chairs from Lauren's office, he muttered in her ear.

'She cheated, made the deal when our forward was lining up for a winning goal, sixty metres out and less than a minute on the clock.'

'If you agreed, it's binding.' She grinned at the usually stylishly dressed man—even in casual clothes on the weekend—now in well-worn jeans, football jumper and that distinctive beanie. And loved him even more.

'You siding with Kaye?' He gave her a hard, lip-smacking kiss. 'I can think of a few bets I'd willingly lose to you.'

She recalled hours of sitting rugged up on cold

benches, being bumped and bruised by excited supporters. She thought of days wasted setting up stalls, being bored and trying to persuade people to buy merchandise or raffle tickets. Now she looked into hungry blue eyes and knew she'd go through all of that in a thunderstorm if he were beside her.

Matt kept a tight hold on her hand as they walked to the stadium, joining an ever-growing throng that bottlenecked at the bridge over the river. He kept telling himself this was for her but that excuse was wearing thin. It was he who wanted to share his enthusiasm for their national game, who wanted to see her lose her inhibitions and cheer with the mob. It was he who wanted her with him when they played in the finals.

It was a full house by the time they bounced the ball for the start and the noise was deafening. For the first time ever his concentration wasn't out there with the players. He watched Lauren, quite prepared to take her out if she became stressed. Instead he saw interest grow as her eyes darted from the field to the big screens and back.

His heart usually pounded at the fierce interaction between players, now it was because she leant forward as they ran, held her breath as they shot for goal and flopped back when they missed. By the fourth quarter, she was on her feet with Kaye every time the lead changed, face flushed and eyes shining. And he didn't care an iota that he missed most of the action on the field.

'A twenty-eight-point win. Our best this year.' Kaye danced up the steps, arms swaying with her scarf held high. 'You must be our lucky charm, Lauren.'

Matt hugged her close 'You are definitely mine.'

Lauren clung to him, treasuring his words. The excitement had been contagious. Her head spun, whether from the buzz of the crowd or the shock of discovering the thrill of the game overrode her inhibitions, she wasn't sure. As if tied to Kaye with invisible bonds, she'd found herself leaping to her feet and calling out phrases she'd never spoken, hadn't known she'd memorised.

Matt was grinning as if he'd been the star forward. Not a smug, I-told-you-so smile; he was genuinely happy for her. Had she been wrong all her life or was she seeing everything through new eyes? And if she had changed because she loved him, why couldn't he love her for the person he was helping her to become?

Monday afternoon Matt decided to grab a chicken wrap on the way back from the bank. Funny how easily he'd adapted to healthier meals and salads. Not funny that in a week he'd be eating alone again.

Lauren. His pulse hiked up, and he quickened his pace as he saw her opening the door of a café across the street. He halted when she spoke to the dark-haired woman entering behind her. She hadn't mentioned meeting anyone.

By the time he'd crossed at the lights and walked along, they were seated at a table studying menus. An old friend she'd caught up with? He wouldn't disturb them; she'd tell him over dinner tonight.

She didn't. She was quiet and withdrawn, claiming fatigue and a headache. Concerned, he persuaded her to take a tablet and go to bed. In the morning he left her sleeping.

Tuesday was no different. She blamed it on the current autumn virus and he had to admit she looked unwell, though she didn't cough or sneeze. Was she depressed thinking of the shrinking time they had left? That he understood.

He'd never considered a cross-country romance. There'd never been a reason to. The idea of seeing Lauren only on weekends was gut-wrenching but better than not being with her at all. Would she be prepared to try?

Alan's text came through as he was driving to work Wednesday morning, and he read the short, concise message in the lift. Apprehensive, and with fingers tapping his desk, he accessed the online morning papers. The small article tucked away in one of the business sections sent his world crashing in flames.

Names weren't mentioned but anyone with determination and knowledge of the company or his father could identify them. Obscure hints were made of illness, legalities and the long-term viability of the business. His temper rose as he researched the reporter, found her profile and photo.

And his fragile faith was obliterated in a torrent of bitterness, far worse than all the other betrayals combined. This was the woman Lauren had been with on Monday, the reason for her reticence since.

She was one of the very few who had knowledge of his father's dementia *and* fraud. What reason could there be for meeting that woman? Why?

His chest heaved, and anger ruled as he reached for his keys. Threw them down, snatched up his mobile, and paced the floor until Lauren answered.

'Matt?'

Diffident and wary. Guilty?

'Who was the woman you were with on Monday?' Grated out without polite niceties.

Her quick gasp sharpened his pain. Her silence exacerbated his temper.

'She's a damn reporter. What did you tell her?'

'You…I'm…'

'Lost for words, Lauren. What am I? A magnet for cheats and liars? Dad, Christine, and now you? Do you have any idea what I…? No, you wouldn't. I can't bear to see you. Don't want to hear your voice.'

He hung up, tossed his phone on the coffee table and sank into a chair, burying his head into his hands. This was it. He'd never fully trust anyone again.

CHAPTER SIXTEEN

LAUREN CURLED UP on his settee, buried her head into his cushion and sobbed at his tirade. How could he believe she'd break her promise?

Idiot, stupid, stupid idiot. She hadn't realised the woman was a reporter until she'd begun to ask about Marcus. Fearing he might be annoyed that she'd been duped into the conversation, she hadn't told him. Things the woman had hinted she knew could only have come from one of the select few people he trusted implicitly.

He hadn't said what the reporter had claimed to know, only accused her of telling family secrets, and she had no way of proving her innocence. Maybe if she had been truthful with him he'd be looking for the real culprit. Instead he'd condemned her without even seeing her, proof his caring had been superficial.

She rubbed the tears from her cheeks, and went to wash her face with a cold flannel. The red-eyed wreck in the mirror gave her no choice.

She loved him so she'd make it easier for him. He didn't want to see her so she wouldn't be here when he came home. She booked a flight, packed her belongings and called a taxi.

* * *

Matt hadn't needed his cousin's harsh rebuke over the phone to know he'd been wrong to call her in anger. Personal confrontation when he could see her eyes and read her expression would have been better. Didn't change the reality. Or did it?

Alan had rung to say he'd done what Matt should have—checked and found out the reporter was ambitious, and not particularly scrupulous in her methods of obtaining information.

He couldn't postpone the morning's scheduled meeting though he came close to doing just that. It was crucial to the company's survival, especially after today's media article. With the prospect of legal proceedings giving him motivation, he blocked Lauren from his mind and went to the boardroom to fight for his and the company's future.

He deliberately stayed late at the office, arriving home to a dark and silent unit. Refusing to acknowledge the sour churning in his gut, he walked in.

I can't bear to see you. Don't want to hear your voice.

His words echoed in his head. He sagged against the door jamb leading to the kitchen area. The table was bare. The vase had gone. Lauren had gone.

Lauren had never felt more alone. She ached for Matt's smile, his spine-tingling touch, and his midnight-blue eyes that could make her pulse race from across a room. She even missed his cajoling her to reassess her relationship with her family.

Knowing he believed she'd betrayed him tore her apart. Knowing she had unconditional support from her friends held her together. Whatever they suspected, they'd never push, would give her all the time she needed until she was ready to confide in them.

On Wednesday night, she cried herself to sleep, reliving his caresses, his kisses. The passion they'd shared. On Thursday she wandered aimlessly for hours, stopping only for drinks and an occasional snack. On Friday morning she went to see her employer and resigned. When she got back to the units, Pete was home so she told him.

'You can't, Lauren. You're the best. You love digging out the solutions where others have failed. You…' Words failed him and his arms flailed in the air.

Lauren shrugged. She'd lost enthusiasm for her work, and her heart hurt every second of every day. Matt didn't want her, didn't love her and had never really trusted her. He hadn't bothered to ring but she'd have blocked the call if he had. His throaty voice was implanted in her brain. She heard it every night as she lay alone in her single bed. Didn't need to hear the reality and have her heart ripped apart even more.

'I'm going to teach.'

Pete made a scoffing sound, and dropped down beside her on the sofa. 'You'll be bored and climbing the walls in a week. And the salary's crap.'

'Private lessons to adults. One on one showing them just the functions they want to use on their own personal computers. I've done it for friends, and they all said they knew people who'd pay for the service.'

'You've thought it through? It's really what you want?'

'For now it's what I need, Pete. Who knows what's ahead?'

Nothing but memories and what-ifs for her. Her throat tightened—it seemed to do that a lot lately—her breath hitched, and she shivered.

In an instant she was wrapped in friendly arms, her head was cradled to his shoulder and his hand made soothing strokes over her back.

'I'd like to find the guy who hurt you and feed the most destructive viruses I can find into his computer system. *And him.*'

She choked up at the thought of polite, pacifist Pete going into battle for her. She felt warm and cared for, knowing he meant it and that the others would back him up. They might not have Matt's name or details of the breakup but he was now the enemy.

Easing away, she stood up and brushed off the few tears that had escaped.

'Save your knight-in-armour mode for Jenny. He

wasn't completely to blame. He'd been betrayed by someone he trusted and circumstances showed me in a suspicious light.'

'Loving means trusting.'

Which again proved Matt didn't love her.

'And the only way is forward. I'll take each day as it comes.'

And hide my torment in the dark nights.

All Matt wanted to do was to cower in a dark corner and lick his wounds. Nothing he'd suffered before had prepared him for the gut-wrenching pain whenever he thought of her, which was almost every minute of every day. He lay awake remembering the nights they'd spent together, reached out for her in his restless sleep on the couch.

The sun was rising as he drove into the city on Monday, an unneeded reminder of last weekend. Telling himself he was better off without her had no effect. His brain kept repeating one word over and over. Why?

Mid-morning he brewed another mug of strong coffee, couldn't bear to drink it in his office. Even with the connecting door shut, he kept glancing that way as if she'd suddenly appear. He walked to the boardroom because she'd never been in there but she came with him now, in his head and his heart. There was no escape.

On the way back, the lift doors opened as he went through Reception and Clair stepped out.

Surprised by her tentative smile when she saw him, he walked over.

'I didn't expect to see you, Clair. You're always welcome, of course.'

'I had to come. Can we talk?'

Her apprehension triggered a kindred unease. That damn article? Duncan had already assured him the reporter's insinuations hadn't affected his opinion at all. There was nothing he wasn't aware of and their association wouldn't change. He was also convinced the people who mattered wouldn't equate Marcus's condition with Matt's aptitude to run the company.

'Of course, this way.' He guided her to his office, and over to the window seats.

'Coffee or tea?'

'Not now. Please, Matt, sit down. This is personal and it concerns you.'

His gut tightened as he obeyed. Lauren? He'd told Duncan she'd returned to Sydney. Not why.

She fiddled with the handle of her bag then dropped it onto the floor. He leant forward and took her hand, shocked to feel its trembling.

'What's wrong, Clair? If there's anything I can do, just ask.'

'It's the other way round, Matt. I came because I'm partly responsible for that reporter's knowledge, limited though it was.'

'You?' He shook his head, couldn't take it in.

A chill seeped into his muscles and he dreaded hearing more.

'Your mother came to our group lunch two weeks ago, first time for ages. We were chatting in a quiet corner and she began to tell me about her problems with your father and his deterioration. I should have suggested we talk later somewhere more private but she was desperate to let it all out.'

The chill became icy. Every cell in his body seemed to shrink and close down. He had a vague awareness of letting go of her hand, of his shoulders slumping.

'She said your father kept telling her things she knew weren't true or dropping hints about special funding for his secret hideaway retirement. She didn't want to worry you or the family with his fantasies, just wanted someone to sympathise with her.'

His mother had confided in a friend because he'd built barriers between them. She'd been overheard and Lauren was innocent. The reporter had been trying to get confirmation or more details. It was as if he heard the facts but couldn't process them through the fog in his head.

'Duncan showed me the article, and this morning I found out the woman who wrote it had been at the venue. I noticed her hanging around, and assumed she was a guest. I'm so sorry, Matt.'

Oh, Lauren, what have I done?

Guilt and anguish raked him, his throat clogged,

and his stomach heaved. Condemnation roared in his head. Sweat dripped down his back, and his fingers balled into fists.

'Matt. Matt, are you all right?'

His mind cleared. Clair was leaning forward, regarding him with deep concern. He shuddered back to reality.

He'd listened to her, heard what *she* said. He hadn't heard Lauren's explanation because he hadn't given her a chance to tell him.

'No. I think I've made the worst, stupidest mistake of my life and I'm not sure she'll ever forgive me.'

'Lauren?'

He nodded, too ashamed to speak.

Clair patted his knee. 'Go and tell her in those exact words. Lauren loves you, Matt, and we women in love can forgive our men almost anything if they love us too.'

Could they? Would Lauren, after his bitter accusations?

Lauren stared at the four family-sized pizza boxes and clutched her fingers in her lap. She'd always begged off the Monday pizza, footy and whatever-you-want-to-drink evenings in Pete and Jenny's unit. Why had she agreed to come tonight?

Because she wanted to prove she could watch an Aussie Rules game without breaking down. And she would as long as she didn't think of the crowded Adelaide oval and being crushed against a warm, muscular body in the crowd.

'So, did you keep that appointment with your boss, Lauren? Has he made an offer you can't refuse to get you to stay?' Jenny leant forward and opened the top box, the aroma evoking memories of the last time she'd been in Matt's office.

'We talked. He wants me to consider freelancing for him whenever he gets a job he thinks worthy of my talents. His expression. Soft soap and flattery. I think he's hoping I'll relent and come back full time after I've had a break.'

'Could happen.'

'I doubt it but the idea of a real challenge now and again is tempting.'

The last one had been and look how that ended. No chance of a repeat. She'd fallen in love and lost her heart to Matt Dalton, irretrievable and never to be reclaimed. The pain would subside and become a dull ache she'd learn to live with.

Matt needed someone to confess to, someone who'd listen, tell him what a drongo he'd been, and offer to help find her. The one person who'd shared all his dreams and aspirations, almost every failure and heartbreak. As soon as he'd finished essential work, he took a taxi to Alan's city apartment, picking up Chinese food on the way.

The food was hot and spicy, and the cold beer from the fridge slid smoothly down his throat giving him courage to begin. He lounged back, crossing his ankles.

'Lauren was my balcony girl.'

Alan stopped chewing and stared.

'You're kidding? I don't remember seeing her that night and she'd have been noticeable even then. *You* definitely never forgot her.'

'No, she was always there, even when I was contemplating marriage to someone else. I didn't realise who she was until I kissed her again.'

He almost lost it as the memory seared his brain. Closed his eyes, picturing hazel eyes full of passion, and a smile that always sent his pulse soaring.

'I'm an idiot, Alan. A blind, insensitive idiot who didn't have the nous to see the truth in front of me or the guts to claim the sweetest prize any man was ever offered.'

His cousin nodded. 'I agree. Now you tell me what happened and we'll work out how you find her, grovel like a lovesick fool—which you'll happily be—and win her back.'

Matt spilled his guts, taking all the blame. He'd cursed himself for not asking more about her life, her suburb, or the names of her friends. She wasn't in the phone directory and he hadn't been able to locate her on social media. Her employer had offered to forward any mail he sent, after justifiably refusing to divulge personal information. Apologetic words on paper could never convey his guilt and remorse. He needed to see her, hold her and beg for forgiveness.

'My last hope is to contact one of her brothers but they'd probably ask why and refuse if I tell the truth. All I know is she lives on the same floor as her friends, in a suburban block of units in Sydney. I didn't bother to ask her anything—'

He jerked upright, beer spraying onto his jeans and the floor.

'The form.' He sprang to his feet, dumping the can on the table. 'Come on—you drive.'

'What form? Where?

Matt was already halfway to the door.

'The personnel form I filed without bothering to read it. Her name and address, contact number in case of an emergency, et cetera.'

Ten minutes later Matt perched on *her* desk and read the form out loud.

'"Lauren Juliet Taylor", her address and mobile phone number. And—' the rush of joyful adrenaline almost tipped him off the desk '—"Peter Williams", her friend in the apartment opposite hers.' He punched the air in triumph. 'I've got where she lives. I've got her friend's number. And with his help, I've got a plan.'

Lauren fumbled in her shoulder bag for her keys as she took the last few steps to the third floor. Her first private lesson had been a success and her next three Tuesday afternoons were taken.

If even half her future clients were as good as feisty seventy-two-year-old Mary—or seventy-two years *young* as she'd claimed—her new occupation would be a pleasure. She'd listened intently, made copious notes in a neat legible hand, and was willing to give anything a go. She claimed making mistakes was part of living.

If that was the case, Lauren was certainly alive, so why did she feel numb inside? There was…

A large vase containing an incredible arrangement of orchids on the landing outside her door. Her foot caught on the last stair. She couldn't breathe, couldn't form a coherent thought.

Orchids: deep reds, yellow with leopard spots, and lilac ones of every shade imaginable. She stumbled forward and fell onto her knees, her trembling fingers reaching out to touch the soft petals, confirm they weren't her imagination.

Tears flooded her eyes. Her heart hammered into life, sending her blood racing to regenerate every pulse point. Orchids. Matt. Linked together in her mind for ever.

'Lauren?'

Broken, rasping voice. Trembling arms clasped her in a strong embrace. Warm lips pressed to her forehead. Disbelief scrambled her brain, and hope fluttered in her stomach.

'Don't cry, my love. Please, don't cry.'

My love. Matt's voice saying words she wouldn't dare to dream. Matt kneeling beside her, his body warm and solid, and his heart thudding under her hand. Matt's fingers lovingly stroking her cheek, and tilting her chin.

She barely had time to register dark shadows under his compassionate blue eyes before he kissed her. Not with the smooth arrogance of the youth, or the competent skill of the sophisticated man. Hesitant, unsure of her response.

She wanted the passionate lover who'd taken her to the moon and beyond, and refused to settle for less. Wrapping her arms around his neck, she tangled her fingers in his hair, binding him to her. She teased him with the tip of her tongue and nipped his lip with her teeth.

In an instant he crushed her against him, chased her tongue back inside with his, stroking and tangling, claiming his rights as her man. His hands caressed her, fuelling fires she'd believed extinguished. His breathing was as ragged as her own.

Voices echoed up the stairwell and he lifted his head, chest heaving, throat convulsing and eyes gleaming.

'Inside?' Rough and barely audible.

Unable to speak, she nodded, and looked round for the keys she'd dropped. Matt picked them up and helped her to her feet. Her fingers trembled too much to take them, and her heart flipped at his unsteady attempts to unlock the door.

He followed her in, stopped just inside gazing wide-eyed at her home.

Her home, where she'd spent six tortured nights berating the fool that she'd been to fall in love with him. Where she listlessly performed necessary chores, and agonised over a solitary future without him.

He stood there as if he were a returning hero carrying his gift like the spoils of war. And the anguish and heartache she'd suffered surged into a torrent of anger at his injustice.

'No.'

CHAPTER SEVENTEEN

HIS BODY JERKED, his brow furrowed, and his mouth fell open.

'You bring flowers and expect what you did to be wiped away and forgotten? You judged me guilty without proof, willingly believed I lied to you.' She retreated as she spoke, torn between aching for him and never wanting to suffer like this again.

'You never trusted me from the day we met. You were willing and eager to take me to bed but never prepared to give anything of yourself. Except your body for your own pleasure.'

'No. No, Lauren. I was…'

'Protecting yourself.'

His features contorted. He raised his hands, blinked as the orchids came into his view, and strode across the room to place them on her book-shelf. He turned to face her, his hands reaching out to her, and his dark beseeching eyes pleaded for understanding.

Her heart clamoured for her to run into his arms, surrender and forgive. But he'd disowned her over the phone, without giving her a chance to explain.

She straightened her shoulders and lifted her

chin. When his hands fell then one rose to rake through his hair, her fingers itched to join it.

Flowers and kisses came easily to him. If he thought he could win her over by...

'How did you get into the building?'

He broke eye contact, and stared at her cream velour sofa with its colourful cushions. Typical Matt, plotting his reply instead of saying what he felt.

'Can we sit and talk? Please, Lauren. I know I've been a drongo and selfish as hell. And the dumbest prize idiot for not admitting even to myself that I love you.'

Her world slammed to a shuddering halt. The air rushed from her lungs, her legs trembled, threatening to buckle, and she leant on the breakfast bar for support.

'No, you don't.' Breathless. Distrustful.

The adoration in his eyes stirred the cold embers in her core, and she scrunched her fingers, wouldn't fold. He'd coerced her so many times. She'd need more than words to risk her heart again.

She moved to the sofa, determined to conceal the effect of the hot tendrils of desire weaving their way to every extremity as he joined her. Leaving space between them, he spread his arm along the back and hooked one ankle over the other knee—a simple, familiar habit that chipped at her resistance.

'Pete let me in.'

This wasn't going the way Matt had planned.

He'd been wrong in so many ways, including persuading her to face her demons while fooling himself about his own.

He'd banked on her being thrilled with the flowers, and melting into his arms. Seeing her on her knees with tears streaming down her face had shattered him.

Her response to his kiss had been all he could have wished for. She cared. They'd talk and she'd forgive him. They'd make love and work out how they could be together.

Lauren had stunned him with her hostile stance and accusation, her flashing hazel eyes demanding he fight for her, and prove he was worthy of her love. Living without her had been hell. Together they could build their own heaven.

'You named Pete as your contact on the company's personnel form I'd filed without reading. I had completely forgotten about it until yesterday. He was tough to convince, but finally agreed to meet me with no guarantees of help. He also threatened to take me apart if I ever hurt you again.'

Her lips curved and he found himself grinning at the image too. He had height and weight advantages but he had no doubt Pete's threat was sincere.

'I have…had trust issues. I never saw my parents kiss or be affectionate, and rarely heard them argue. Came home one evening and it was full on. He'd been having affairs for most of their married life. She put up with it because she wanted the life-style he provided. I was gutted at their hypocrisy.'

'That's why you left Australia.' She leant to-wards him. The tightness in his gut eased, and he ground out the rest.

'He used his business premises for rendezvous.'

'The bedroom?'

'I've never been in there. It's a tangible reminder of his adultery, and I swore I'd never be like him. That's what always stopped me from kissing you in the office.'

She shuffled a bit closer, and covered his out-stretched hand with hers. As always with her touch, his heart beat faster, and his temperature rose. He needed to get the truth out, have no more secrets. Then he could hold her again.

'Apart from the woman in London, I knew oth-ers, male and female, who believed fidelity was outmoded. Faithful couples seemed to be a minor-ity, or maybe my pride saw it that way as proof my father wasn't so contemptible. If I didn't believe in love their relationship wasn't abnormal.'

He took a chance and moved towards her. She stopped him with a hand on his chest, eyes wary and sceptical.

'You didn't want any of the photos.'

He caught her hand, raised it to his lips and kissed her palm. Rejoiced in her quivering reac-tion, and his own. Regaining her trust was paramount so he fought the craving to enfold her in arms and kiss her the way he had in the hall.

'*They* were for you. I ordered another set, which should have told me how special the evening with you was, and how much you already meant to me. It came the day after you left.'

His thumb began an automatic caress of her knuckles. When she didn't pull free, he closed his eyes and took a long breath.

'I refused to believe in love even though I knew couples who proved me wrong. My experiences, including suspicion of my father's computer deception, gave me little reason to trust in any sphere of life.

'Then you walked into my office and all my resolutions collapsed. I fell in love, probably had ten years ago and hadn't been mature enough to recognise it. I stubbornly ignored the reality when we met again.'

Her smile grew as he spoke, her beautiful hazel eyes glowed, and his resolve crashed. He gathered her into his arms where she belonged, setting his world right. A different aroma, as alluring as the other, filled his nostrils. He brushed his lips across her forehead, and if his heart beat any faster, he'd short circuit.

'Matt?' She raised her head, a tiny furrow creasing her brow. 'That reporter…'

'She overheard my mother talking at a luncheon and started digging. I should have come home and talked to you. Instead I let my past rule my head. I couldn't admit, even to myself, that only you had the power to break my heart. My stupid pride almost destroyed us both.'

'She said she knew Clair, implied things about your father. I swear I told her I didn't know what she was talking about.'

'I believe you. I'll never doubt you again, my darling. I love you. With all my heart and all that I am.'

He kissed her deeply, lovingly with no reservations. Cradled her as close as humanly possible, only breaking away to breathe. Found the air clogged his throat at the love shining in her eyes.

'I love you too, Matt.'

He slipped from the sofa onto his knees in front of her and held her hands in his.

'Lauren Taylor, you are sweet and courageous, and I'll love you 'til my last breath and beyond. I'm yours, only yours, for ever. Marry me?'

Lauren couldn't speak. Her head spun as if she'd drunk too much champagne; the electrical zing from his fingers through hers was zapping along her veins at airship speed. Her already pounding heart threatened to burst from her ribcage.

The love in Matt's eyes wrapped her in an aura of soft warmth, a haven where there were only gentle caresses and love. A special place of devotion and commitment. For two.

'Yes. Oh, yes, please. I love you, Matt. I'm yours, now and for ever.'

He let out a roar of triumph, scooped her up and swung her round. She clung to him as her joyous laughter mingled with his. When he stopped, his kiss was gentle, reverent. He laid his forehead to hers.

'I ache to make love to you, darling, but I promised Pete and Jenny we'd go and tell them the good news.'

'Confident, huh?' She tried to sound stern; it came out husky and adoring.

'Optimistically hoping I hadn't misread the signs when we were together, the passion when we made love. No way was I going to walk away unless you looked me in the eyes and swore you never wanted to see me again.'

He kissed her again then set her on her feet and nuzzled her neck.

'We'll still have all night.'

Matt missed the earliest flight home in the morning, caught the next and went straight to the office. He stood in the doorway, taking in the expensive décor, the stunning views and his father's top-of-the-range desk. He didn't need all this to define himself, never had.

Knowing Lauren loved him gave him a goal to be better than he was. It was time to lay the first ghost to rest. He strode purposefully across the deluxe tiles, through the first door and into the bedroom.

It was neat, tidy and impersonal. Overwhelming sorrow shook him as he thought of how much his father had risked for the brief encounters in this cold place. He thought of his mother knowing the truth and living a lie.

Closing his eyes, he conjured up Lauren's lovely face as he'd kissed her goodbye, hair tousled, eyes shining. Together they'd face the uncertainties ahead. Together—a couple united by a vow to share life's fears and sorrows, its triumphs and joys.

Leaving youth's judgement and bitterness behind, he scrolled for his mother's number. From today he'd make up for the years of estrangement.

That evening, Matt held his mother close without censure and, for the first time in nine years, embraced his father. The hug he received in return filled his heart with love and relief.

Marcus was almost his old self and pleased with the gift of his favourite wine. As Matt opened it he regretted missed opportunities like this, reflected on his culpability then let it go. The past couldn't be changed but it could be left behind if they were all willing to face the future.

'I'm in love with a very special lady and she's agreed to marry me.' He couldn't keep it in any longer, and was elated at how good the words sounded out loud. Even more so when his mother hugged and kissed him and his father shook his hand.

'She's flying in from Sydney on Friday and I'd like Lena, Mark and the boys to join us here for lunch on Saturday to meet her.'

Before he left he had a private talk with his mother, pledging his and Lauren's support in caring for his father. They'd sworn together to keep their knowledge of his father's infidelity a secret from her, saving her any more pain.

Finally acknowledging that loving someone meant accepting their faults and weaknesses, he put his arm around her. Holding her close, he regretted the years they'd lost.

'I was young, arrogant and so very wrong to keep distance between us for so long. If I hadn't you'd have been able to confide in *me* and that reporter would never have had a story to write.'

'You have your father's pride, Matthew. Promise me you won't let it come between you and Lauren.'

'I promise. She's more than I deserve, and is willing to help us keep Dad at home with you as long as possible.'

She wrapped her arms around him and he clung tight, grateful that he had the chance to make amends and heal the rift between them.

Mid-winter, the twenty-third of June. Lauren woke before the alarm, stretched and smiled at the blue skies behind the treetops outside. Sunshine as predicted for her winter wedding day, though not even a cyclone could mar the occasion. Tonight she'd be Mrs Matthew Dalton.

She threw back the covers, and ran to the shower, leaving the door open in case he rang early. He did, but by then she was perched on the side of the bed, wearing her dressing gown, and combing her towel-dry hair.

'Happy wedding day, my love. I missed you.' The sound of his voice, gravel rough from sleep, was her favourite way of starting each day.

'Me too, Matt. I'm lost in this bed without you.' She lay back into the pillows, wishing he were here beside her in the Fords' guest suite.

'Wasn't my idea to spend the night apart. Clair and our mothers ganged up on me. Never going to happen again if I can prevent it.' The low growl in his voice skittled up and down her spine. He'd only begrudgingly agreed after she'd said it would please the older women.

'I'll make it up to you.' She dropped her tone, trying for seductive, laughed when he growled again.

'You will, my love. I kept myself awake compiling a list.'

She quivered with delight, imagined ticking off each item. 'I love you, Matt. Four o'clock is a long time away.'

'Longer until we're alone. Then we have two weeks, just you and me where no one can find us.'

Someone tapped on her door.

'I have to go. I've got company.'

'Look in the bottom drawer on my side of the bed, darling. I'll see you at four. I love you, Lauren.'

Her mother peeped in as she ended the call. Along with thrilling Matt and Lauren with the offer of their home and grounds for the wedding, Duncan and Clair had invited her parents to stay with them for the event.

Accepting there would always be differences between herself and her family had allowed her to form a real bond with them. Matt had ensured no one on her guest list was absent, and hotels and guest houses in neighbouring towns were filled with relatives and friends from interstate.

'You're awake. Happy wedding day, darling.' Her mother hugged and kissed her, and sat on the edge of the bed.

Do you want to come for a walk with me, Clair and the dogs after a quick breakfast? It's going to be chaotic once the trucks start arriving with the marquee, and everything.'

'Give me ten minutes and I'll see you on the veranda.'

As soon as her mother left Lauren dived over the bed, pulled the drawer open, and took out a small black box. She gasped with joy at the delicate yellow pendant and earrings. A real full orchid and two orchid centres preserved in resin with their true colours.

Matt's message, handwritten on the small white card, was memorised, never to be forgotten. Every word of the text she sent him came from her heart.

It didn't turn out to be so long after all when the hours were filled with the walk, meals and watching the lawn areas being transformed into a perfect venue for her dream wedding. She agreed to a hair stylist but did her own make-up, her hand as steady as her heartbeat. And every two hours she slipped away to be alone when Matt called, their secret pact to keep in touch throughout their special day.

Marcus and Rosalind arrived and she shared a quiet time with the two sets of parents. Her future father-in-law had no idea he'd been spared prosecution because of his deteriorating condition and the fact that no withdrawals had been made from the secret accounts. Everything had been transferred into the company files and all due taxes paid with interest for late submission.

Dalton Corporation had a new direction, the contracts for the new project had been signed last month, and Matt was the official CEO. He and his colleague in London were negotiating the sale of his flat and his shares in the consultancy firm.

The way everything fell into place, and ran smoothly to favourable solutions, sometimes scared her. Then she'd look into Matt's eyes, and know that, whatever troubles they encountered, he'd be there to love and support her, and smooth their way forward.

It was ten minutes to four. There was a chill in the air, and all areas were dotted with outdoor heaters. Somewhere in the garden Matt was waiting for her, as impatient as she was to make the vows that would join them for life.

She saw the rows of seated people waiting as her father escorted her across the veranda, looked beyond them to the decorated arch where the celebrant stood with...

Everything bar the man who'd turned towards her became lost in a haze that surrounded her. Matt, who'd taught her to let her true self shine, and showed her she was worthy of being loved. There was only Matt and his irresistible smile, his electric touch and those oh-so-persuasive lips drawing her closer. Only his midnight-blue eyes growing misty as she reached him. Only him, his gentle kiss and whispered words as he embraced her.

Matt would never find the words to express the emotions that rippled through his body when he turned to see Lauren at the top of the veranda steps. A vision in white was inadequate. She was gorgeous, stunning, and wearing his wedding gift.

This beautiful woman who'd captured his heart and soul as she helped him save his father's company and reputation. His own special angel who filled his days and nights with love and laughter.

Their eyes locked and the world disappeared as he willed her to his side. He acknowledged her father's traditional greeting automatically, his focus on Lauren's dazzling smile. Drawing her into his arms, he kissed her soft lips and whispered how much she meant to him.

They stood face to face, hands joined. Ten years ago he'd asked for a prize and claimed a kiss. He might not deserve her, but today he was claiming the best, the sweetest, the most loving woman as his for ever.

* * * * *

If you enjoy office romances,
look out for the next 9 TO 5 *title,*
MISS PRIM AND THE MAVERICK
MILLIONAIRE
by Nina Singh—on sale next month!

REUNITED BY A BABY BOMBSHELL
by *Barbara Hannay*

*Griffin Fletcher never imagined he'd see his
childhood sweetheart Eva Hennessey again, but now
he's eager to discover her secret—one that will
change their worlds forever!*

Read on for a sneak preview:

A baby. A daughter, given up for adoption.

The stark pain in Eva's face when she'd seen their
child. His own huge feelings of isolation and loss.

If only he'd known. If only Eva had told him. He'd
deserved to know.

And what would you have done? his conscience
whispered.

It was a fair enough question.

Realistically, what would he have done at the age of
eighteen? He and Eva had both been so young, scarcely
out of school, both ambitious, with all their lives ahead
of them. He hadn't been remotely ready to think about
settling down, or facing parenthood, let alone lasting love
or matrimony.

And yet he'd been hopelessly crazy about Eva, so
chances were…

HARLEQUIN® *Romance*

Next month, Harlequin® Romance author

Marion Lennox

brings you:

Stranded with the Secret Billionaire

Rescued by a brooding stranger…

Jilted heiress Penny Hindmarsh-Firth has set her
broken heart on escaping high-society city life.
But she's trapped by floods in the Outback, and a
handsome stranger on horseback comes to her rescue!

After a betrayal shattered his life Matt Fraser
withdrew from the world—but he can't deny Penny
refuge. This secret billionaire is reluctantly intrigued
as the society princess begins proving there's more to
her than meets the eye…

**On sale April 2017,
only from Harlequin® Romance.
Don't miss it!**

*Available wherever Harlequin® Romance books
and ebooks are sold.*

www.Harlequin.com

HR74429

Dragging in a deep breath of sea air, Griff shook his head. It was way too late to trawl through what might have been. There was no point in harboring regrets.

But what about now?

How was he going to handle this new situation? Laine, a lovely daughter, living in his city, studying law. The thought that she'd been living there all this time, without his knowledge, did his head in.

And Eva, as lovely and hauntingly bewitching as ever, sent his head spinning too, had his heart taking flight.

He'd never felt so sideswiped. So torn. One minute he wanted to turn on his heel and head straight back to Eva's motel room, to pull her into his arms and taste those enticing lips of hers. To trace the shape of her lithe, tempting body with his hands. To unleash the longing that was raging inside him, driving him crazy.

Next minute he came to his senses and knew that he should just keep on walking. Now. Walk out of the Bay. All the way back to Brisbane.

And then, heaven help him, he was wanting Eva again. Wanting her desperately.

Damn it. He was in for a very long night.

Make sure to read...
REUNITED BY A BABY BOMBSHELL
by Barbara Hannay,
available April 2017 wherever
Harlequin® Romance books and ebooks are sold.

www.Harlequin.com